# Their Lady Gloriana

Starla Kaye

ISBN 978-1-936556-00-7



Published 2011 republished 2015
Printed by Black Velvet Seductions Publishing
A division of Savage Publications

Visit us at:
www.blackvelvetseductions.com

www.blackvelvetseductions.com

## Chapter One

*Middlemound Castle, England, June 1272*

"Riders come, my lady! Two of them," a guard called down from the parapet to Gloriana where she stood in the gardens. "They bear the King's banner."

She raised her head toward the guard and felt chills spiraling up her spine. News. Bad news. She sensed it to her soul. "Allow…" she had to clear her throat before she could finish. "Allow them entry."

The two maids working with her to gather vegetables looked worriedly at her. One of them hurried to her side. "Are ye all right, my lady?"

*No.* She was far from being all right, but she refused to show weakness to her servants. They'd witnessed enough of that in the past. She forced a reassuring smile and handed the younger woman the basket she'd been holding. "I'm fine, really. Twas just a surprise."

With that said she walked around the corner of the keep and heard the unusual silence in the bailey. She noted the dozen or so soldiers who had been training there now stood still, tense and cautious. All had heard rumors from traveling tinkers that the last battle of the Crusade had ended. All were awaiting the return of their lord and the men who had gone off to fight with him. Like her, though, none were overly eager to have Geoffrey Stewart back. He was a hard man, cruel and vicious at times…especially to her. No, she did not look forward to hearing news that her husband of barely three years would soon be home.

Her red-haired bailiff, Sir Gerald, strode toward her. He'd become her fierce protector during her second difficult year with Geoffrey and had often dared to come between his lord and her. She'd worried that Geoffrey would one day lose the last of his patience and kill the man, and that worry returned now at seeing her knight's expression.

"He will *not* harm you again, my lady," Gerald vowed. His nostrils flared and cords stood out in his thick neck.

"You must not put yourself in harm's danger, Sir Gerald." She held her chin high, tried to keep from showing the tremble of alarm spreading through her. "Your lord would never truly hurt me." Twas a lie and they both knew it. He'd seen her bruised face on occasion; he'd seen her walk gingerly after yet another sound lashing. Yet it wasn't the beatings that hurt her the most. No, her husband flayed her even worse with his harsh tongue. Gerald's brow furrowed and his gaze darkened. She noticed the way his hands fisted at his sides. But before he could respond, they were interrupted by the pounding of hooves across the wooden drawbridge.

Gloriana stiffened her spine, prayed her knees would not fail her, and waited for whatever news the messengers were to deliver.

The small contingent of soldiers in chainmail and bearing the king's banner rode between the rows of silent men straight to her. She fought against rubbing her nervous stomach and sucked in a breath to calm her racing heart as she ran her clammy hands over the sides of her gown.

She watched as Gerald stepped forward and stopped next to the lead soldier. Both men nodded in acknowledgment. Without saying a word, the man extended a rolled parchment. "You may find food and ale in the hall," Gerald offered. He waved a page over. "Tend to their horses."

The men glanced toward Gloriana. She had to swallow down a lump of distress before she could force a hint of lightness to her tone. "Please go inside, as Sir Gerald said. The maids will see that you are fed and given drink."

The tension eased from the soldiers' expressions and they began dismounting. Her own men watched in continued silence. She wished they would go about their business again, but she knew they were waiting for her to read the message. They waited to be told the news that might affect the castle.

As the king's soldiers moved away, Gerald extended the parchment toward her. She shook her head. Her hands were trembling too much, her thoughts scattering in fear of hearing that her husband would be here within a day or two. She wasn't ready to see him again, even if she had no choice. "Nay, I would ask you to read it to me."

He glanced around. Gloriana was aware the silence remained heavy around them. Nearby, soldiers, villagers and servants waited for the news the king's men had brought.

"Please," she prompted, her voice quavering. With a nod of

acceptance, he untied the parchment. The paper crinkled loudly as he unrolled it. His eyes widened as he read it over quickly and then frowned at her. "Tis two items of importance, my lady. Are you sure you don't wish to read it yourself?"

She shook her head, and then commanded, "Read it."

He pulled in a breath and said with grimness, "Lord Middlemound will *not* be returning, my lady. He died over a month ago in the battles." Gloriana's knees gave out in her shock, and one of the nearest soldiers hurried to steady her. "Not returning? Dead?" The words left her mouth in a whisper. Relief filled her instead of sadness. But that was wrong. She would beg forgiveness for such an awful sin in her prayers later.

A quiet hum began around the bailey as word spread quietly but speedily of their lord's death. She sensed relief from her people as well. She could pick out not one word of unhappiness or regret in the soft din of voices. How very sad it was that one should die and no one expressed sadness at the death. But, there it was, Geoffrey Stewart had been a man no one would miss. Certainly not her.

Gerald caught her attention once more and said with clear unhappiness, "King Edward has decreed that you will marry Lord Montrose upon his arrival at Middlemound. He is travelling here with his men and with Lord Middlemound's men."

The buzz around her became louder as the additional news spread. She heard the mixed opinions, sensed the mixed emotions. She'd seen Lord Montrose once at Edward's court. What she remembered was a big man, even taller and brawnier than Geoffrey. He'd had striking dark blue eyes and a hardened look to his handsomely carved face. Yet not one of the women who'd danced with him at the ball appeared to fear him. No, most all but drooled over him. She, of course, had been with Geoffrey and had not danced with him, nor even been allowed very close to him.

Gerald watched her. "Lord Montrose is a fierce warrior, I've heard. They say he's the very devil in battle, but a good leader."

*A devil in battle…fierce warrior.* Nerves twisted and twined in her stomach. Geoffrey had been fierce, too. A devil as well.

"Those who have sworn allegiance to bear a sword at his side do so with pride." His awe toward the man rang clear in his words and in his eyes. "He was widowed long ago and has a son. Fostered out by now, I'm sure." He shifted uneasily. "I've never heard that he treats a woman poorly."

Again she thought of the man she'd seen at court, a man that none of the ladies had seemed to fear. Dare she hope… Gerald's unspoken promise replayed in her mind, "He will *not* treat you poorly."

It was much to take in: learning she was widowed and betrothed again in the same moment.

"Mayhap you should go lie down, my lady," the soldier still holding her arm said gently. "That is much news to deal with."

She blinked out of her musings and nodded as he released her. "Mayhap you are right." She glanced at Gerald. "Does the missive say when we should expect Lord Montrose?"

"Nay, but I will question the messengers. Mayhap they have an idea of when they will arrive."

Needing time alone, Gloriana nodded and walked toward the keep. She noted the sympathetic and relieved expressions on the servants she passed; their uncertainty as well. She suspected many had heard of Lord Montrose's reputation as a warrior, but she doubted any knew the man himself. He could be as hard a leader as Geoffrey had been. Had not Gerald just told her of his fierceness in battle? To be such, would not the man have to be cruel at times, demanding much of himself and of his men?

Her footsteps slowed as her thoughts tumbled about. Mayhap Montrose was a strong warrior and yet a good and loyal leader, not a cruel one like Geoffrey. How did his intensity as a leader affect him beyond the battlefield? Gerald had not heard that Montrose treated a woman poorly. Yet what a man could do behind closed bedchamber doors… She had far too much experience with the horrors of that.

She shivered at the memories, but shoved them back. Instead her mind recalled watching Montrose from across the ballroom. She saw the politeness, the care he had shown the women he'd danced with. Would such a man turn around and be cruel and demanding in bed? She didn't think so. She prayed that would not be so. She did know that he had gotten under many women's skirts at court, as those rumors spread quickly. Surely that meant he most likely was nothing as vile in bed as Geoffrey. But it could mean that he, too, would find his way into more than just her bed. She could probably live with him seeking other women's beds, since she was already used to that. Still, she would like him to give her a baby.

Gentleness curled through her. Tears misted her eyes. How many nights had she lain awake recovering from Geoffrey's cruelty and longing for something to give her life meaning? How many times had she ached to hold a wee babe in her arms? Longed to feel its softness, to know its loving trust in her? She would wrap her baby in all the love she had within her. She would protect it with her life. Having a baby to cherish and care for would give her the strength to survive anything.

***

*North Yorkshire, England*

Thomas stood next to the River Ure while his horse drew in water beside him. He looked out over the valley leading to Middlemound Castle. A faint breeze swept over him carrying the scents of sweet clover from the patches bursting with flowers nearby. Along with it, he drew in the heavy smells of sweat; his own and that of Rowan, who stood quietly a few feet away. He imagined all of his men—including his new men—smelled equally as unpleasant after these last long days of travelling.

"I suppose we should all bathe in the river before we head toward Middlemound." He said the words without hazarding a look at his first knight. He dared not think about the roughly handsome man being naked anywhere near him as long as his other men were nearby. Even the mere thought of Rowan in all his hard-muscled glory, naked, had Thomas's cock showing interest.

Understanding the problem, Rowan said, "Aye, I'm sure everyone there would appreciate not smelling the stink of our many days on the road." He turned to head back to where they'd camped last night. "I'll pass the word." He hesitated before walking away. "I'll go into the river farther upstream."

As he heard his friend move off, Thomas felt the strain of arousal slip away as well. He and Rowan had discovered an appreciation for one another quite by accident almost half a year back. An appreciation that had quickly led to some of the hottest sex he could ever remember experiencing. At first Thomas had been shocked, not sickened or appalled, just surprised. He'd always loved being with women, quite lusted after them actually. He had a hearty appetite for sex and he'd never had any complaints from his more than willing bed partners. Yet he'd never been drawn toward a man before that time with Rowan. He still wasn't drawn toward other men. Only Rowan fired up his need to make love to a man.

His glance shifted to Castle Middlemound in the distance. It was impressive, sprawling over a large piece of prime land. Even from here, he thought the gray stoned main structures were three stories high along the east and north sections, and not far from its curtain walls stood a village with many houses. This was a holding of great value. It still surprised him that King Edward had commanded he hold Middlemound and marry Geoffrey Stewart's widow. He'd met Stewart on more than one occasion at court and disliked him. He'd distrusted the man even more on the battlefields in Tunis. His death did not bother Thomas at all. But being ordered to wed the man's young widow did. He tried to remember seeing her at King Edward's court, but couldn't place her. Yet he was certain Lord Middlemound would not have married a woman displeasing to the eye. Not that her appearance would matter to Thomas. He'd bedded his share of homely women and been satisfied. He and Lady Middlemound need only be agreeable in bed together to please him. He would not seek out relief from maids or find a mistress. He'd been faithful to his first wife during the short time they'd been together before her death in childbirth. He would be faithful again.

He heard Rowan's deep voice telling the men to bathe in the river and his thoughts returned to Rowan. Although he'd tried to convince his first knight to take over Montrose castle from him, Rowan had refused. He'd also refused to accept a holding of his own offered to him by King Edward. Rowan wanted only to become Thomas's first in command at Middlemound. He didn't want to leave Thomas. While Thomas was certain there could be problems ahead, he was grateful for the man's loyalty both as a soldier and as a lover. For if Gloriana Stewart couldn't fully satisfy his hungers in bed, at least Rowan could.

***

*Middlemound Castle*

*They were coming. Soon. Dear God, what was she to do?*

Lady Gloriana stood in front of one of the small windows in the chapel and peered out. She'd fled up here after Gerald had talked to the king's men and learned Lord Montrose and his soldiers were camped not far from the castle. She'd wanted time alone to find some way to make peace with the latest changes in her life. But her time was quickly running out.

Even now she heard the powerful hooves of the many horses passing over the wooden drawbridge. She looked out the window and saw the large group of men merging with the castle's guards in the bailey. Her stomach fluttered with nerves. She could barely draw in a breath. This fear, this caution and timidity sickened her. She hadn't always been this way. Her life with Geoffrey had done this to her. He'd battled down her self-worth, her dreams of having a happy family, and her natural zest for life.

She refused to continue on like this. She needed to find the strength to face this new marriage to this war-hardened warrior. She had to make him respect her where Geoffrey never had. She had to make him allow her to be the keep's chatelaine as was her rightful duty, although Geoffrey had never allowed it. Most of all, she had to endure relations with him until he got her with child.

Determined, she stepped away from the window, smoothed down her gown, and gathered her courage. She left the comfort of the small chapel and headed for the stairs. With each step, she considered bolting to her bedchamber and locking herself inside. *Keep moving. Don't be such a weakling!*

Her steps faltered as she neared the bottom of the circular stone staircase. The great hall rang with the sounds of joyous reunions. The families of the Middlemound men, who had been gone for nearly a year, happily greeted the returning soldiers. Men who had stayed behind to guard the castle welcomed the soldiers as well. She heard unfamiliar voices too, no doubt Lord Montrose's men. And then the deep tone of another unfamiliar voice. It rang with authority, with power, much like Geoffrey's voice had. Yet something about it drew her instead of repelling her as his voice had. Something about it called to her woman's place, and she felt warmth spreading there. The reaction surprised her, but there was no time to think about it now.

"Lady Middlemound," Gerald said, snagging her attention. "Lord Montrose asks to see you."

She couldn't read Gerald's expression, couldn't tell if he was unhappy about the situation or resigned to it. At least he didn't appear angry or overly protective of her. She gave a slight nod and joined him at the foot of the stairs.

The deep rumbling voice she'd heard drew her focus to the raised dais. Two men stood there drinking cups of ale, talking, looking over the hall full of people. Two such different—and yet the same—men. The darkly handsome man she'd seen across the ballroom at King Edward's court and an almost equally handsome man with blond hair both glanced her way as if sensing her presence. Neither smiled. Both seemed to study her, their gazes sliding from her carefully braided hair to her suddenly aching breasts, down her best jade green gown to her slippered feet. Then as their gazes lifted, her breath caught at the obvious heat in their eyes. *Lust.* She'd seen it in Geoffrey's eyes many times, but never directed at her. No, he'd lusted after nearly every other woman in the castle and nearby village but never for her.

Gerald held her arm by the elbow and guided her to the dais. "Lady Middlemound, my lord." He released her and nodded toward the two powerfully built men. "Lord Montrose, my lady, and Sir Montgomery, his first knight."

"Thomas," Lord Montrose said and stepped down in front of her. He towered over her by at least a foot. His breadth and brawn made her heart race. Yet she didn't feel intimidated by him as she had been by Geoffrey. His dark blue eyes assessed her from beneath thick dark eyebrows, pinched together in thought. Yet they were not cruel eyes. "You may call me Thomas." She bobbed her head and had the oddest desire to run her fingers over the dark stubble on his face. Or gently touch the long, thin white scar on the left side of his face running from just to the side of his eye to his jaw. Or to smooth them over his full and tempting lips. All such notions made her blush, made her look away. "Gloriana," she whispered.

Then the other man stepped down next to Thomas. As she glanced up, he gave her a crooked smile. "And you may call me Rowan."

She blinked at him and felt her heart race even more. Where Thomas had a head of thick, wavy black hair that brushed his shoulders, Rowan's hair was dark blond, chin-length and straight. His eyes were brown and appeared both interested in her and slightly amused. "Gloriana," she repeated, more forceful this time.

Thomas cleared his throat to capture her attention. "We have much to discuss. In private."

"Yes," she said, again feeling her stomach flutter with nerves. "Yes, we do." She nodded toward the stairs. "The solar would be good."

As Gloriana climbed the torch-lit stairs in front of him, Thomas watched the gentle sway of her hips beneath the green gown. She was a tiny woman, delicate, fragile for a man such as him. His first wife had been a woman of fair size, not that he'd minded. They hadn't been in love and he'd never grown to love her, but she had pleased him outside of the bed. She had managed his household well. His people had respected her, as had he. Yet there had been no lustful feelings between them.

The sweet swell of Gloriana's buttocks held his gaze. And he recalled how generous her breasts had looked barely contained in the low neckline of her gown. He'd hardened as he'd stared at them, as he'd fought a desire to lower his head and her gown so he could taste of the tempting mounds. He remained semi-hard as he climbed the stairs behind her. He hadn't been with a woman in months and the need to have a soft, pleasing woman beneath him once again was almost overwhelming. This small woman drew him as no other before her ever had. He was both uneasy with that and glad, for they were to marry. Soon.

He heard Rowan's heavy footsteps behind him. The two of them had talked about Edward's decree during their long ride from Tunis. Both of them had concerns about the matter. Neither wanted this marriage to affect their deepening relationship, but both knew it would. Thomas wouldn't give up Rowan. Somehow he had to make both situations work.

"She's a pretty one," Rowan said quietly. "I'm thinking twill nay be a hardship to have her as a wife."

Thomas considered what his friend said, wondered about the tone of his voice. Rowan bedded women, but he'd told Thomas once that his attraction for women grew less as they grew closer, as their love grew stronger. Yet he was certain he'd heard a touch of envy in his lover's tone. As if he, too, well appreciated the petite beauty thrust into their lives. He wasn't sure how he felt about that. Later he'd ponder the idea.

Gloriana stopped in a doorway, waited with a smile that looked forced. "Geoffrey's … I mean, *your* solar, my lord."

As Thomas strode closer, her eyes widened and held a hunted look. *She feared him.* Because of his well-known reputation for being a tenacious, often merciless warrior on the battlefields? Because of rumors spread through Edward's court of his numerous liaisons with women after his wife's death? He wondered. Or did she fear him just for being a man?

He'd seen how Geoffrey treated women in the towns they'd traveled through on the way to Tunis. Cruel was putting it lightly. He'd even interceded once, making them enemies from that moment on. Had the man been brutal with Gloriana? His hands knotted into a fist. No doubt.

The idea sickened him.

He stepped by her quickly so as not to make her any more anxious than necessary. *Patience.* He would have to draw on his limited patience and settle her down before they married.

"I … I understand you," she said uneasily, "are to marry me."

Thomas went to stand by the large, scarred wooden desk and let her frightened words roll over him. Rowan walked beside him, giving him a look of understanding. He'd picked up on her fear as well. Rowan, too, had witnessed Geoffrey Stewart's vicious side when it came to women. He, too, had despised the older man and had stepped in to defend a helpless young woman.

She eased into the room, although she stayed near the door. She hovered there, giving him the impression she wanted to be there in case she needed to run from them. If ever a woman needed a protector, it was this one. He sighed. He could be her protector, *would* be her protector. Rowan, too, would keep her safe; there was no doubt of that in his mind.

As he watched her, he felt outraged at what she might have suffered at Geoffrey's hands. The man had no respect for women, would have had none for his wife. He saw a hint of curiosity in her eyes as she looked from him to Rowan. Those same eyes warmed with sensual interest for the barest of seconds before she blinked it away. The woman had a passion that she didn't know what to do with, that she feared letting anyone know about. The lovely Gloriana needed a man to teach her the softer ways of intimacy and to unleash her hidden desires. He felt challenged to peel away the layers of fear and distrust, to soothe her worries, and to gain her trust. He looked forward to it.

He met and held her gaze. "Aye, King Edward wants me to hold Middlemound for the crown. It is a valuable asset both land-wise and with people here known to be loyal to him." Trying to look less intimidating, he leaned back against the desk. "He wishes us to wed as quickly as possible. He believes that as soon as word spreads about Geoffrey's death, men wanting to lay claim to Middlemound will come from near and far. They will want not only the castle and its lands, but also you."

"Me?" She blinked in puzzlement. "I have no value, other than having been Geoffrey's wife." The sadness in her expression, that she appeared to believe such nonsense, tore at him. He wasn't sure what to say. Rowan answered for him. "You are wrong, Gloriana. You have great value."

She cocked her head slightly and worried her lower lip for a second. "Geoffrey didn't value me." "He was a fool," Thomas stated in anger at the same time Rowan said the same thing. Her pretty face grew pink. "Although it is sinful to speak badly of the dead…or of one's husband…I agree." Thomas smiled at her spark of spirit. He hadn't smiled in a very long time and was surprised he could even still manage it. Evidently his smile wasn't as comforting as it should have been because she shifted uneasily. A crease of concern furrowed her brow.

"Forgive me, my lord," she said quietly, fidgeting with the folds of her skirt.

"For speaking the truth? Nay, there was nothing sinful in what you agreed to. Geoffrey Stewart was a vile man, disliked by most people who crossed his path. Feared by women unfortunate to come anywhere near him." Thomas slammed his mouth shut and wished he had watched his tongue better. *She* was one of the women who had feared Stewart, one of the women who had been, he was certain, seriously mistreated by him. The man deserved to spend eternity in the fiery depths of Hell. To his surprise, she straightened to her full barely over five-foot height and thrust out her chin. "Aye, I feared the wretched man every day of our life together. But, know you this, I will *not* endure that kind of life again. No man will ever treat me that way again." Thomas felt his chest swell with admiration. Some men would not allow a woman to speak so boldly to them. Many men expected complete submission. He was not one of them. He appreciated honesty and someone who held strong to their beliefs. Aye, with time and patience, they would make a good couple.

"You will never need to fear me, little one." He meant it. She brought out the fierce protector in him. He would never allow another person to harm her in any manner. That chin thrust out even farther. "I might be small in stature, Lord Montrose, but do not mistake me for being incapable."

Rowan gave a chuckle and quickly covered it with a cough.

"Incapable of…?" Thomas questioned, curious to what she was referring. She stopped fidgeting with the sides of her skirt and looked directly at him. "Geoffrey didn't believe I was capable of acting the chatelaine for the keep. He didn't think anyone would listen to me, take me serious because of my size. But he was wrong! I've acted as chatelaine ever since he left nearly a year ago. My people listen to me, respect me. I *want* to continue with that duty."

Thomas had to admit that he'd been concerned about her handling the normal duties of a lord's wife in the running of the keep. She appeared little more than a child, and she brought out his strong need to protect those weaker than himself. He would try his best to give her some free rein, within reason.

He gave a nod. "As much as I see that you are capable of handling, Gloriana."

Her lips pursed in annoyance for a second, and then she seemed to accept his statement. Her gaze held his once more, but her creamy cheeks grew pink. "Geoffrey also thought me incapable of pleasing him in bed." She looked away, curling her hands into fists. "In truth, when we were first married, he never gave me the chance. Then … well, then I lost any interest in doing so."

She shifted her gaze back to him, anger flashing in those grass green eyes of hers. "He never pleased *me* either."

"More fool than we'd first thought," Rowan said with a snort of disgust.

Thomas glanced sideways at his friend and, again, wondered what Rowan's feelings were for this intriguing woman. He felt a second's jealousy. Because he would be Gloriana's husband and didn't want another man thinking sexually about her? Or because Rowan might be interested in Gloriana and no longer in him? Or because Gloriana looked as heatedly at Rowan as she did at him? Who was she drawn to?

"Trust me, my lady, you will definitely find pleasure in our marital bed," Thomas said with determination.

She cocked an eyebrow. "I heard many tales of your conquests at court, Lord Montrose. Often those tales are mere overblown rumors." Her face hardened. "I'd heard tales about Geoffrey, too, before we were wed."

Thomas saw Rowan stiffen beside him. He knew Rowan's need to defend the weaker was even stronger than his own. Had Geoffrey not already been dead, Rowan would have taken his blade and cut off the older man's cock for what they both suspected he had done to Gloriana.

"You will come to no harm in my bed," Thomas assured as gently as he could. "I promise you that."

"He's a man of his word, Gloriana. You can trust him to take care of you, to be gentle in loving you, or to be passionate when you desire it." Rowan glanced at Thomas, silently acknowledging what happened between them.

She looked curiously at them. "Good friends as well as lord and first knight. You watch each other's backs. Tis good, that."

Thomas didn't want to go deeper into the subject. He merely nodded and then straightened from the desk. "We will say our vows on the morrow."

Her eyes widened and she sucked in a shallow breath. "As you wish, my lord."

***

The keep was quiet as Thomas lay awake in his temporary bedchamber. He'd lain in bed for the last hour thinking about tomorrow, about saying marital vows to Gloriana. Uncertainty curled through him. It was clear she'd experienced some manner of abuse from her previous husband. She didn't truly want another husband, but she had no choice in the matter. He, too, was reluctant to wed again. His first marriage had given him a wife who tolerated him and his physical attentions. They'd been friends of a sort, no more. She had been completely submissive to him, had never questioned him about anything, and had never spoken up for herself.

He stretched and thought about how Gloriana had seemed at first timid, fearful even, but then she'd dared to speak against her brute of a husband. She'd insisted Thomas let her fulfill the normal duties of a lord's wife; be the chatelaine. He'd agreed, with reservations. She was so slight, appeared so in need of protection. He could easily envision her being taken advantage of, even hurt in some way while trying to tend to her duties. He would not stand for either. He would watch her carefully, and only if she could truly prove herself would he give her free rein in the role.

His thoughts turned to James. It had been far too long since he'd seen his son. In truth, he'd seen very little of his ten year old son. When Sarah had died in childbirth, he'd not even been there. He'd been off battling on behalf of King Edward. His sister and her husband had raised James until now, although he'd made sure James knew he was his father. Now that he planned to settle here at Middlemound and train soldiers for Edward rather than going off to war, it was time to bring James to live with him.

Frowning into the darkness, he wondered if Gloriana was infertile. She'd been married to Stewart two years before the man had gone off to the Crusades. Surely the man had tried to get her with child. He frowned even more. Even though he barely knew her, he hated the idea of Stewart taking her to his bed. He hated thinking about the man known for his cruelty with women driving into her delicate body with no care for her. He would be as gentle as he could with her. Hopefully she would soon find that he could give her great pleasure, and, hopefully, she would free the passion he sensed within her.

His body was too tense now to consider falling asleep. His cock throbbed, demanding attention. For a second, he reached down and stroked the hard rod. But he wasn't interested in finding relief that way, not when Rowan had settled into a bedchamber at the far end of the hallway.

Thomas pulled on his braies and headed out into the semi-dark hallway. The only light came from torches in holders on the stone wall. He padded barefoot toward the chamber Rowan had claimed. He needed Rowan tonight and hoped Rowan needed him as well.

He hesitated in front of Rowan's door. What if one of the maids was with him? He'd seen Rowan leading one up here earlier; he'd known what they'd had in mind. It hadn't bothered Thomas then. Yet he would be disappointed if the young woman was still with Rowan.

The wooden door opened, startling him. Rowan stood naked before him with a slow smile sliding over his face. He motioned Thomas inside.

Relieved, Thomas strode into the chamber. His glance took in the rumpled bed and the candles burning on the bedside tables. He smelled sex in the air and felt a second of jealousy. As it passed, he faced his first knight, the man who had protected his back nearly as many times as Thomas had protected his. He nodded toward the bed. "Mayhap you don't want..."

"Hell yes, I want!" Rowan countered, sounding almost angry. "I want a good pounding."

Pleased that this much hadn't changed, Thomas felt the tension drain from him. "Good."

Rowan cupped Thomas's head with his calloused hands and leaned toward him. Their lips met with familiarity. Thomas raised his hands and wove his fingers into Rowan's chin-length hair, pulled him closer. Heat flared through him, need, demanding in its intensity. He slid his tongue along his lover's lips until they parted. Then their tongues parried as they'd done so many times before.

Rowan skimmed a palm over Thomas's bare chest and deepened the kiss. Thomas had kissed many a woman in his years but none kissed with Rowan's fiery enthusiasm. Rowan took his mouth hungrily, with an almost feverish desperation. Thomas's cock hardened and pressed between them, throbbing, aching for relief. His balls swelled as the kiss went on. Rowan didn't give him a chance to catch his breath. Yet somehow his thoughts turned to Gloriana. He recalled her rosebud mouth, the passion that had flashed in her eyes when she'd stood up for herself. Would kissing her be… Rowan rubbed his lower body against him and commanded his attention. Thomas's focus returned fully back to the man he'd come to see. His body thrummed with the powerful need for more.

His chest heaving, Rowan pulled his head back. His nostrils flared. "I've missed this." He pushed Thomas's braies down, enough to free his hard cock. Grinning, Rowan gripped it, worked the pulsing shaft slowly with his strong hand. "I've *really* missed this."

Thomas groaned. His hips rocking as his cock was pumped repeatedly. Rowan's other hand cupped Thomas's balls. He closed his eyes and groaned. "God's teeth, I'm so hard," Thomas bit out.

He couldn't take any more. He shoved Rowan's hand away before he lost all control. "Now. Right now!"

Rowan grinned, clearly proud of having driven him half mad with need. He turned and walked to the bed. The dim light from the candles teased over Rowan's toned body, over the taut ass that drew Thomas.

He pumped his dick and watched Rowan settle onto hands and knees. God, he wanted in that ass.

Looking heatedly at him, Rowan wiggled his ass. "I'm ready for that pounding now."

Thomas moved quickly behind Rowan and took a second to stare down at the butt he so loved. Pre-cum leaked from his cock, making his lover's eyes widen and making him lick his lips. If they didn't both need this so desperately, they'd take more time. Thomas would let Rowan lick that cum; let him suck long and hard on his cock. And he'd return the favor before they got down to actually fucking. But he ached to be inside Rowan too much right now.

He coated a finger with the pre-cum before finding Rowan's puckered anus and sliding his finger inside. Rowan kept his head turned away, and Thomas watched in fascination and pleasure as his finger disappeared.

He gritted his teeth and probed deeper still. His jaw tight with tension, Rowan craned his head back to look at Thomas. Their gazes locked and Thomas drove a second finger inside as well.

Rowan's eyes glazed over; his face tightened. "Work me," he gritted out, shoving back in demand.

Thomas twisted his fingers, pulled them nearly out, and then shoved them deep again. His cock throbbed. He couldn't do this much longer, or he would shoot off, and he'd rather be buried deep in Rowan's warm hole when he did.

"Fuck me!" Rowan bent down to rest his head on his forearms. "Pound me into the bed!"

Wanting to do it as much as Rowan wanted him to do it, Thomas guided his thick cockhead into Rowan's anus. He inched forward, letting his friend adjust. When he heard the quiet moan, felt the release of tension, he thrust all the way inside.

"God, yes!" Rowan squirmed and pushed back. "Do me. Do me now!" The commanding words served to make Thomas's cock grow even more. He needed control and he took it, pulling his shaft almost out while Rowan growled in protest. Then he plunged hard, deep. Being surrounded by the tight space felt so good, so warm. He repeated the action and watched Rowan clutch the linens, heard him groaning, straining at the invasion of his ass.

Thomas drove harder and faster. Sweat beaded his upper lip, his chest. His heart thudded as he burned for release. It had been too long, nearly a month, since they'd had the chance to be together like this. He groaned, fought for breath.

"More. Fuck me harder!" Rowan's body was shuddering, as Rowan moved back and forth, frantic in his desperation.

Thomas's eyes lost focus and his mind spun. *Deeper. Deeper still.* He held Rowan's hips and pumped for several more agonizing minutes. Waves of pleasure pulsed through him. He shifted slightly and the new angle forced a rough, guttural cry from the man beneath him. It ignited the fire within him, building it higher and higher. He couldn't last much longer. He panted. "Uh, oh God!"

Rowan shoved his ass back at him. "Do it! Now."

Thomas's energy was draining away. He couldn't think about anything beyond finding release. He had to have relief! He tightened his hold on Rowan's hips and rammed as deep as he could a final time.

His breathing stopped as he froze in place with his cock buried to the hilt. Then with a shuddering sigh, he shot his hot seed in Rowan's tight passage.

They collapsed next to each other as they'd done many times before. Thomas turned to his side. He knew Rowan liked having him watch as he worked his own rod. Thomas watched as Rowan's hand pulled steadily on his cock. His handsome face was covered in sweat, grimacing in tension. A vein pulsed in the side of his neck. Thomas knew that him watching excited his lover even more, made him stroke the swollen cock faster, made him breathe deeper. In truth, observing his lover do this excited Thomas as well. His limp rod showed signs of interest again, but not enough. The intense fucking had taken the strength out of him for now.

His face pinched in strain, seeming to hold his breath, Rowan finally cried out almost as if in pain. Thick ropes of cum shot upward and then glazed over his hand. After a second he closed his eyes and drew in a long calming breath.

When Rowan finally settled back to the moment, Thomas leaned over and kissed him tenderly. As their lips met, he thought again about Gloriana. Was he being fair to her by marrying her? Was he being fair to Rowan? What he and Rowan did was unnatural by society's eyes, but necessary to both of them. As lord of a substantial holding, he was expected to have a wife. The people of Middlemound expected him to wed their lady. He would do so. But what about Rowan? Could they keep the relationship they had? What would Gloriana do if she ever learned of it?

"I'm thinking you're a lucky man to wed her," Rowan said, interrupting Thomas's troubled thoughts. "I saw the fire that burns within her, just as you did."

Thomas wondered about his friend's comment, and he remembered the odd look he'd caught as Rowan watched Gloriana at sup. They'd have to talk about her later, but now he was tired. Tomorrow would be a long day, a trying one.

"I do not want to hurt her." Thomas climbed from the bed and pulled on his braies.

"You won't." Rowan sat up and looked seriously at him. "She will be lucky to have you in her life."

"I can't give you up." Thomas noted how Rowan's gaze had settled on his chest, shifted lower. If he didn't leave the chamber now, he might end up staying here the night. Already his cock was showing more determined life again.

"Nor I, you," Rowan released a tense breath. "Tis best you leave while you can."

Thomas nodded and walked to the door. He glanced back at his lover, but Rowan's eyes were closed. His brow furrowed in thought. "We'll make this work. Somehow."

## Chapter Two

The sun had barely risen by the time Rowan dressed in his tunic and braies. He jammed his low boots on and glanced back at the rumpled bed. It reeked of sex from his time spent with Marie, a maid who had worked her wiles on him. She hadn't had to do much. He'd been ready for driving his cock into a willing woman. He'd been sure to give her great pleasure, but his needs had surpassed what she could give him, at least that time. He wasn't complaining and would probably seek her out again. Yet he'd needed Thomas. Thank God his friend had come to him late in the night.

He left the chamber and headed downstairs. Thomas's door was closed, and he heard the muffled sound of snoring. At least his friend was getting some rest. This would be a big day for them all. He knew Thomas had mixed feelings about marrying Gloriana. He was concerned as well. The marriage would only add to the complicated life he and Thomas led. He didn't want to give up their relations. He'd been with only a couple of other men before Thomas, but none had compared to Thomas. He'd been Thomas's first male lover and he hoped to be his last.

Lost in his thoughts, he nearly plowed right over Gloriana as she stepped out of her bedchamber. She gave a gasp, and he caught her to keep her from falling. The instant his arms went around her, he felt a jolt of awareness. His heart raced. His cock swelled. Blinking in shock, he all but thrust her from his embrace.

She, too, looked surprised. Her pretty face blushed in embarrassment. "I'm sorry, Sir Rowan," she gushed, stepping farther away. "I wasn't paying attention."

"I'm sorry as well." He tried to calm his body, tried to see if she'd been struck by the same startling sensations as he. "I was thinking about something else."

"I trust you slept well." She smoothed down the sides of her gown. It was another green one, which emphasized her emerald green eyes that could both hint at past pain and warm with concern. Now they watched him in confusion.

Without thinking, he said, "I hardly closed my eyes."

She cocked her head and the waist-length blonde hair moved just enough to make his fingers ache to weave their way through it. "Are you feeling poorly? Was there something wrong with the mattress?"

He couldn't tell her that thoughts of Thomas had kept him awake. That he'd wanted to find Thomas's room and pin his lover to the mattress and ram deep into his upturned ass. He couldn't tell her that he'd also spent a fair amount of time puzzling over the attraction he'd felt for her yesterday. An attraction that had grown even more alarming when he'd held her only seconds ago.

Instead, he gave her a weak smile. "There is just much on my mind, Lady Gloriana." He wondered if adding her title would help him put distance between them. She returned his smile and the gentleness of it stabbed at his heart. Like Thomas, he wasn't a soft man. There'd been very little kindness or gentleness in his life. But her softness made him want to pull her to him once more. *Thomas's bride.* Remember that.

Biting back disappointment, he nodded toward the stairs. "Shall we go break our fast?"

"Tis still early, but I'm sure we can find some bread and cheese in the kitchen." She hurried away as if relieved.

They didn't speak again until she reached the bottom of the stairs. The great hall was filled with people, some still sleeping on mats on the rushes, some just waking and starting to move around. Snores and quiet whispers met his ears.

"Thomas will make you a good husband," Rowan said, determined to think of her only as his friend's future wife. He didn't want to keep noticing the gentle sway of her bottom, or how her plump breasts filled out her bodice. He didn't want to inhale the scent of her, the hint of a flowery soap she must have used. "I'll admit I'm more than a little worried." She looked up. Her gaze searched his for something, but he didn't know what.

"I've known Thomas for almost a year now." He remembered the day they'd first met on the battlefield. Thomas had ridden his huge black destrier straight into the middle of a group of men who had him pinned. Thomas had already suffered wounds himself, but he had raised his sword and had quickly saved Rowan's life. "There's not a man I respect more.

I would give my life for him without a thought."

She didn't look reassured. Her gaze moved about the large hall, moving over the many soldiers. "I know of his reputation as a warrior. All here at Middlemound do. But Geoffrey was a warrior, too. A hard one."

"Stewart was a sadistic, brutal warrior with no sense of honor. He took what he wanted by any means. He would cut a woman down as easily as he did a man." At her gasp, he slammed his mouth shut. *Good God, what had he been thinking to say such a thing to her?* "I apologize, my lady. I should not have—"

"No. I'm sure what you said was only the truth." She stiffened her slight shoulders. "I suffered at his hands many times and am not at all saddened by his death."

Then she realized what she'd said and paled. "I shouldn't have said that."

"Again, it was only the truth spoken."

"My lady, I will get you some bread and cheese. Mead, too." A reed thin young woman walked closer and blushed as she looked at Rowan. "For you, Sir Montgomery, as well?" "Aye. I would appreciate it." He gave her a smile and her blush turned up a notch before she scurried toward the kitchen. Gloriana studied him and then said, "You've got a very nice smile, Sir Rowan." Her demeanor softened and she laughed. "I fear you'll soon have all of my young maids trailing after you."

He was long used to gaining the attention of most any woman he encountered. It both pleased him and annoyed him. He enjoyed the softness and passion of a woman. But he enjoyed the hardness of a man, too and the intensity of a man in the throes of wild passion. Like Thomas.

Just the thought of Thomas naked and pleasuring him made his cock begin to harden. The thought of Thomas bent over so he could drive into his ass made it swell even more. Yet when he glanced down at Gloriana, he longed to see her spread out before him on his bed. He wanted to suckle her breasts and slide into the warmth of her body.

As if she saw the heat in his eyes and understood the reason, she stepped back and tried to change the subject. "I heard someone say King Edward offered you a castle to hold, but you turned it down." She headed toward the dais and the long table there for the lord, his lady, and the first knight.

Rowan followed her, nodding in acknowledgment at a few of the men now rising and moving to tables to break their own fasts. He sat in the chair next to her. "Tis true. Even Thomas offered me to hold Montrose Castle for him. But I'm not interested in a holding of my own. Not now, anyway." The maid rushed back with two mugs of mead. Another carried trenchers of bread and cheese. Neither young woman seemed in a hurry to leave them. He didn't encourage either to stay. His interest lay only with Gloriana.

After they reluctantly moved away, Gloriana broke off a piece of bread and asked, "Why not?" "Thomas needs me." Rowan sipped at the mead, watched her nibble on the bread. "He has warred for nearly a dozen years, travelled constantly. He wants to settle down, but he's unsure if he can really do it." She eyed him curiously. "What about you?"

He wasn't sure what he wanted, other than to stay here for a while. He'd been on his own longer than Thomas. As the bastard son of the Duke of Remington, he'd been a thorn in the powerful duke's side. He'd been acknowledged but never accepted by the duke's wife or his family with her, so he'd left where he'd been fostered at eight by his father and found another castle and lord to take him on. The lord had been hard on him, but he'd learned much and had become the seasoned warrior he was because of him. He'd drifted around from battle to battle, from castle to castle. He'd been a favored warrior by Edward for several years and more so after he and Thomas had joined together, fighting side by side. Being with Thomas was as close to settling down as he'd ever come. He wasn't ready to give up their friendship.

"Rowan?" she questioned when he took too long to answer. "I don't mean to pry, if it makes you uncomfortable. I was only curious."

As he stepped off the stairway not far away, Thomas caught his attention. At the sight of his lover, Rowan felt a similar jolt of awareness as he'd experienced holding Gloriana. He shared a look with Thomas and relaxed.

"As I said, Thomas needs me for now. And I'm content to be his first knight. I would give my life for either him or you."

***

Thomas had awakened with a sense of unease. His first thought had been to go find Rowan. He yearned to have the man's mouth wrap around his cock and work it well. But he hadn't dared go down the hall again now that the day had broken, so he'd dressed with the knowledge that later this day he would wed Gloriana. He would take her to their marital bed. He would not ask her to suck his cock, at least not yet. He would find satisfaction by thrusting into her soft woman's body, though. He'd be gentle at first, not frighten her or abuse her. But, hopefully, they would find mutual pleasure. He would at least give it to her. If he still needed more, he would go to Rowan once she slept. He'd been thinking about both of them as he walked down the stairs. Then he'd picked out the low rumble of Rowan's voice amidst the other voices in the great hall. His nerves had calmed. Until he stepped onto the hall's floor, looked toward the dais, and found Rowan sitting there with Gloriana. Instantly he'd stiffened. He recognized the knotting of tension in his body as jealousy. It had been a long time since he'd felt the emotion. What he didn't know, though, was whether he was jealous of the calmness in Rowan's expression as he sat close to Gloriana, talking quietly, or if he was jealous of the gentleness in her eyes as she studied his friend.

Then Rowan gave him a slight nod and heat flared in his eyes. It was the same heat that had flared when Rowan had demanded Thomas pound into him last night. He relaxed then and moved in their direction. He headed for the hard-muscled warrior who was his lover and for the soft, petite woman who would be his wife. And with each step closer, he felt a more over-powering need. For Rowan? For Gloriana?

"Good morn, my lady." He walked in front of the dais and tried another smile for her. It came easier this time, and she didn't seem as unsure of it as yesterday.

She held tightly to the mug in her hands. "Good morn, my lord."

"Have you instructed the cooks about the wedding feast?" Thomas looked toward the doorway to the kitchens, frowning when he didn't hear much noise coming from there. For a large feast as was normal for a wedding celebration he would have expected many people to be bustling about by now.

"I wasn't sure… Nay, I have not, but I will." Gloriana shoved back her chair and started to get up, blushing at apparently having failed at her duty.

Thomas shook his head, still frowning. "Though this be a second marriage for each of us, I would still have there be a celebration. The people need it. They need to see this as a joining of not only you and me, Lady Middlemound, but also of your people and mine."

She blushed even more. "Yes, I suppose you're right. I'll speak to the cooks immediately." She stood, and then faced him. "But there will be much to do."

He sighed, understanding her concern. Although it annoyed him to put it off, he said, "We will wed on the morrow. That will give everyone enough time to make preparations."

Relief spread over her face, as if she'd just escaped the hangman's noose. The notion only served to irritate him. "But we *will* wed, Gloriana. Do *not* think otherwise."

Now her small chin lifted and a spark flashed in her eyes. "As you order, my lord." With that, she turned and strode briskly toward the kitchens.

Rowan stood to face him, his jaw clenched. "It seems you rub each other wrong. I wonder how that will bode for your marriage."

"She expects to be the chatelaine, which means she needs to handle the duties. Arranging for the feast should have been one of them." Thomas had been hungry when he came downstairs, now he was only irritated. "Mayhap this is all wrong. Mayhap I should refuse being lord of Middlemound and be content with only holding Montrose."

"And mayhap you're being a fool."

Thomas heard people moving and talking all around the hall, felt the eyes of many resting upon him and Rowan. He didn't wish to argue with his first knight here in front of everyone. In truth, he didn't wish to argue with his friend at all. He was just having trouble adjusting to all the changes in his life, changes he had no choice but to go along with. He wanted control of Middlemound, the powerful and important castle. He wanted to stop spending his days riding from battle to battle, sleeping nights on the hard ground. He wanted a home to bring his son to at some point. And he wasn't really opposed to marrying Gloriana. It was just that he hadn't had a woman in his day-to-day life in a very long time. When he pulled out of his musings, he found Rowan watching him. The flash of anger in his expression had disappeared. He nodded toward the stairs and raised his voice enough to be overheard, "Should we go to the solar, my lord? Discuss the strategy of uniting the Middlemound men and the Montrose men?"

They'd already thoroughly discussed the matter, of course. Thomas knew what Rowan was really talking about. His friend knew that he was frustrated, that he needed a release from the tension threatening to turn him into a crazy man. Anticipation crawled through him. "Aye. There is much we need to discuss."

***

Gloriana gave the orders to prepare a great feast for the next day's wedding celebration. The cook and maids had taken the orders with mixed feelings, which she had understood. Her people were nervous about the change in their world. No one quite knew what to expect of the unsmiling, hard-edged warrior to be their new lord.

They seemed to like Rowan who had already become friendly, to a certain degree, with Middlemound's people, in particular a young maid or two, but all were worried about her. She'd tried to reassure her staff that all would be fine, that she did not fear Lord Montrose.

She left the kitchen in relief, stopping in the doorway to rub at her anxious stomach. She didn't actually "fear" Thomas, and she hoped she wouldn't make a miserable showing in his bed on the morrow. Relations between her and Geoffrey had been very basic, at least based upon whisperings of sexual encounters she'd heard maids discussing. Some of the things she'd heard made her blush. Some made her question the actual possibility of doing such contortions. Some things had made her lie awake many nights wondering, feeling excited, yearning to have such an experience. Not with Geoffrey. No *never* with him!

A shudder went through her. It hadn't taken long after their marriage for even Geoffrey's mere touch to make her cringe. Nor had it taken long for his "touches" to become harsh, painful. And then…

She forced the horrible memories aside. He was dead, thank the good Lord. While Thomas was bigger, more muscular, tougher, she didn't get a sense of cruelty from him. There was something sad in his eyes, something vulnerable. She wasn't sure she should trust her instincts, her beliefs that he wouldn't treat her in such demeaning ways. But she did. And she thought about how the very sight of him seemed to start a fire low in her body. Odd, but Rowan, too, excited her, which could definitely be a problem.

Behind her the cook started delivering orders about what foods to be prepared, what vegetables needed to be brought from the garden and in front of her the hall became more and more active, louder. The soldiers were all up and about now, some breaking their fasts, some heading outside for guard duties or preparing for the day's training. She glanced toward the dais and didn't see either Thomas or Rowan.

"Lord Montrose and Sir Rowan went to the solar, my lady," Gerald said. "If you were looking for them, that is." He studied her a second, appearing concerned. "Are you sure..." She cut off her self-assigned protector's question with a raised hand.

"All will be fine, Sir Gerald. Do not worry so about me."

He gave a curt nod, but she knew her bailiff would continue watching out for her. It pleased her as much as it worried her. She looked toward the stairs. "I'm sure you have duties to tend to with all the new men here. And I need to speak with Lord Montrose...I mean Lord Middlemound."

Gerald gave her an understanding look. It was difficult to make such an adjustment so quickly, even though the instant King Edward had given Thomas the castle to hold, it had become his, title and all. As she would become his property on the morrow. She called upon her inner strength and walked toward the stairs. She wanted to talk with Thomas, tell him that preparations for the feast were underway. It was important to her that he not see her as incompetent.

When she approached the door to the solar a couple of minutes later, she found it closed. She hesitated in the semi-dark hallway. She brushed nervously at the sides of her skirt. Maybe this was a mistake. Maybe she should talk to him later. There were many other duties she should be seeing to now. Yet she didn't move away. She wanted to get this conversation over with.

Startling her, she heard Rowan talking with Thomas in low tones. A funny feeling fluttered in her stomach. She liked the sound of his voice, husky and calming. She liked the sound of Thomas's deep, rumbling voice as well. Both made her heart race in a way no other men had ever caused. She worried her lower lip, curious at how she was drawn to each of them.

"Tell me what you need, Thomas," she heard Rowan say. His voice sounded different than she'd heard before, even huskier.

Should she walk away? No. She really wanted to talk to Thomas. But should she knock first? Or should she just open the door and peek in to see if it would be better to come back at another time?

She inched closer to listen against the wooden door, wanting to hear more, wanting to have more to base her decision on.

"Suck my cock," Thomas gritted out. Gloriana's eyes widened and her breath caught. *Had he said what she'd thought he'd said?*

"God's teeth, I need your mouth on me."

*Oh my!* Her face heated. Her woman's place tingled. He had!

"Then you shall have it," Rowan answered with determination.

Gloriana couldn't stand not finding out what was happening inside the room. Heart racing, she carefully opened the door but an inch and peered around the edge. The startling sight in front of her nearly made her gasp. Thomas stood in front of the large wooden desk with Rowan kneeling at his feet. The strikingly handsome blond pulled Thomas's braies down, freeing a long, hard cock that took her breath away. *Good heavens! It would* never *fit inside her.* Geoffrey had been considerably smaller. Stunned and impressed at the same time, she watched Rowan take hold of the shaft and lightly squeeze it. He didn't seem at all repelled at touching the thick cock. She had felt only disgust when Geoffrey had forced her to take his much smaller rod in her hand. It had barely grown from the squishy limp state, which had angered him. He'd made her suffer because she'd failed him…or so he'd told her each time.

As she watched Rowan continue stroking Thomas's shaft, it appeared to grow even larger, even harder. Then he bent forward and trailed the tip of his tongue over the top, and then around the head. *Heavens, the rod looked even bigger! No, it would* never *fit inside her.* Yet she felt a rush of desire spreading through her.

Her glance shifted from Rowan's actions to Thomas's face. His hands were braced on the desk and gripping it tightly. His face contorted as if in pain. Was Rowan actually hurting him? Should she intervene? Her heart raced in concern.

"Don't tease me," Thomas said on a groan. "I need… I need…"

Rowan pulled his mouth away and looked up at his friend. "I know what you need. Be patient a bit longer." Thomas gave a low growl as Rowan again leaned down and slowly swirled his tongue around the cockhead for at least another minute. Thomas appeared to be grinding his teeth together, gripping the desk so hard his knuckles turned white. Gloriana couldn't stop watching.

She'd never known men would do this. She should probably be sickened by the idea, but she wasn't. Her body was reacting as well. Her breasts ached. Warmth settled between her legs and she felt beads of moisture forming there. She had an almost overpowering urge to reach under her skirts and dance her fingers over her lower lips. She'd once done such a wicked thing when she'd lain in bed one night recalling what a maid had talked about that day without knowing she'd been listening. It had been something very naughty one of the soldiers had done to her. Even now just at the thought of it…

"Do it!" Thomas snarled, pulling her from her heated musings. "Suck me. Now!"

Her thoughts scattered and she peeked around the door again. Thomas held the back of Rowan's head and pressed him down until his mouth opened over the cockhead. *Was he going to put that sizeable cock in his mouth? How? Would it really fit?* She couldn't imagine being able to open her mouth that far.

Her heart pounded while she watched Rowan take the length into his mouth, at least several inches deep. At the same time, he cupped Thomas's balls and fondled them. Geoffrey had never allowed her anywhere near that odd little sac beneath his cock. What did it feel like? Her curiosity was running amuck and she absolutely could not look away.

Thomas groaned and arched upward, forcing Rowan's mouth to take even more of that length. And, amazingly, Rowan did. *Good heavens! There had to be at least five or six inches in his mouth!* She opened her mouth; certain such a thing was not possible for her.

Her face flamed again. What was she thinking? This was all so far beyond anything she understood. *Walk away! This is not something I should be observing. It's private. Wrong, not natural.* But that notion didn't feel right, either. They were not hurting anyone by doing this. And it certainly didn't bother her...other than to play havoc with her own body's new desires. She ached like she'd never ached before. She wanted to be touched, to touch as well.

Thomas groaned again and drew her attention. He still held Rowan's head and now his eyes were tightly closed. His powerful chest rose and fell beneath the tunic he wore. With each second that passed, he appeared to suffer more pain. Again she worried about him.

Merciless, Rowan sucked and pulled at Thomas's cock. He moaned, too, although he didn't sound as if he were in pain. No, it was a pleasurable sound. He massaged Thomas's precious balls, the caresses seeming almost gentle. He moved his mouth up and down the shaft, faster and faster, slower, then faster again. Her heart raced faster and faster as well.

Within seconds, both men were moaning, straining, panting. Both looked to be in some kind of pain. She really should step inside the room and... And what? She had no experience with this.

Finally Thomas stiffened, seemed to not even breathe. Then, as Rowan sucked even harder on his cock, Thomas groaned out in near anguish, "Oh God! Oh God!" He collapsed against the desk, his chest heaving as he sucked in air.

She felt slightly lightheaded herself after all she'd seen, after her own strange feelings of arousal.

While she tried to calm her breathing, she watched Rowan's throat work as he swallowed the juices that had flowed into his mouth. At last he sat back on his heels and sighed in contentment.

"Better?" Rowan asked, looking up at Thomas.

Thomas gave a nod. "Aye. Tis what I needed. For now."

*For now?* Gloriana stood quivering, amazed, intrigued. She couldn't imagine what else they might do. Or had Thomas meant they would do this same thing again? Or would he go to his knees before Rowan and suck on his first knight's cock? Would Rowan's cock be as large as Thomas's? As small as Geoffrey's? No, she doubted that. Still, she would very much like to see Rowan's cock. Which, of course, was wrong of her.

Before she could think more about the matter, she heard heavy footsteps on the stairs. Someone was coming! Panicked at having anyone else catch Rowan and Thomas in such an intimate state, she shoved the door open, strode inside, and shoved the door closed behind her.

As both men looked up in shock, one still on his knees and the other with his braies shoved down to his knees, she waved her hands frantically at them. "Get up, Rowan! Pull up your braies, Thomas! Someone is headed in this direction!"

Rowan got to his feet and gave her a crooked smile. "You saw us, didn't you? Naughty, naughty." He chuckled and moved to sit in a chair a couple of feet away. "God's teeth, the idea makes me damn hard."

Gloriana glowered at him, ignored the way her face flamed. "Stop that!"

Then she focused on Thomas, who was pulling up his braies and straightening his tunic. "We can talk about this later," she said. She had a number of questions. Well, mayhap she couldn't ask them, shouldn't ask them.

Thomas cocked a thick, dark eyebrow. "You are not alarmed by what you witnessed?" he asked cautiously.

Footsteps grew closer. "This really isn't the time to discuss the matter," she hissed, glancing anxiously at the closed door. She was relieved that both men were now dressed.

"Gloriana," he pressed. His expression was serious, worried. With a huff of disgust, she said, "No. I wasn't." Rowan grinned. "Tis quite a woman you've lucked onto, my friend." Thomas glowered at him, and then held her gaze for a second. He still looked worried.

Deciding it was best to get away from them right now and think about what she'd observed, Gloriana turned back to the door and opened it. Sir Gerald stood there with one of her soldiers, who was about to knock and looked startled as she pulled the door open. She motioned them into the room and hurried out.

***

The chapel was filled from wall to wall with people, which Thomas knew was out of the ordinary. Usually only the priest, groom and his escorts, the bride and her maidens would be there for the ceremony. All others of the castle would wait for the celebration in the great hall. Yet today was the exception. Villagers, servants, and Middlemound soldiers he hadn't yet met, along with his soldiers from Montrose, took up every seat on the few benches and stood packed shoulder-to-shoulder behind the benches and around the sides of the small space. He'd been surprised when he'd walked in with Rowan, who would serve as his only escort. He'd been waiting anxiously for a good half hour for his bride to appear. His nerves were getting more frayed by the second. And he was sweating beneath his tunic both from the situation and from the heat. No doubt he wasn't alone in feeling misery at the heat of the day.

"She'll be along soon," Rowan reassured him, just as he'd tried to do every few minutes.

Thomas started to give him a frown when they heard a commotion outside. The conversations around the room stopped. Every head turned in the direction of the chapel's door. His stomach tightened. He hadn't seen or spoken to Gloriana since the odd encounter in the solar yesterday afternoon. He'd had duties to attend to, matters to settle with several of the villagers. She'd been busy with the preparations for the feast today, and then she'd retired to her bedchamber before he showed up in the hall for a late sup. He'd worried about what she'd seen between him and Rowan. He'd wondered if she would speak of it to one of her men; to Sir Gerald, who seemed to be her great protector. He'd almost expected to be rousted from his bed in the middle of the night and …

Marie, the maid Rowan had mentioned that he favored and, apparently, a friend of Gloriana, stepped into the doorway. Long, dark hair fell past her shoulders and brown eyes danced with spirit as she looked in his direction. Then she spotted Rowan and blushed before smiling. She started walking toward the front, but Thomas gave her little additional notice. Gloriana stepped into the doorway on the arm of Sir Gerald, who studied Thomas with narrowed eyes. He clearly had to earn this seasoned soldier's trust, especially with his lady. Although not used to having to prove himself to anyone, Thomas found that he admired the man. And then he forgot the man.

Gloriana in a green gown that hugged her body from the low neckline to her slender waist before flowing easily around her legs took his breath away. He actually sucked in a breath and nearly forgot to breathe again. Dear God, she's beautiful! With each step she took in his direction, her waist-length blonde hair swayed behind her and her breasts bounced and demanded his attention. In fact, there wasn't an inch of her that didn't call to him.

"Easy, man," Rowan cautioned in a whisper, that sounded amused. "You cannot grab her and take her to the floor here in front of all and God." He chuckled. "Tempting as that might be."

"Almost beyond tempting," Thomas muttered. He glanced at his friend, wondering about the hint of envy in Rowan's tone. Yet it was more sympathy than anger he felt. Although Rowan might be interested in Gloriana, Thomas was the man who would be marrying her.

The first part of the ceremony passed by in a blur. Thomas got through the priest blessing him as the groom. He half-listened to the older man introducing him and Gloriana to those in attendance as a couple to be married by God's law. And he heard the priest begin the wedding challenge. It was at this point that Thomas came out of his daze and hesitated. Was this what he really wanted to do? Did he have a choice? Should she have a choice rather than being forced to marry him?

Clearing his throat, the priest repeated the question to him. "Thomas Lancaster, Lord of Montrose and of Middlemound, wilt thou have this woman to be thy wedded wife, to live together after God's ordinance in the holy estate of matrimony?"

"I will."

The priest heaved a sigh of relief. "Wilt thou love her, comfort her, honor, and keep her, in sickness and in health and, forsaking all others, keep thee only unto her, so long as ye both shall live?" Again Thomas hesitated. He would not take a mistress, not seek another woman's bed. But what of Rowan? He...

To his surprise, Gloriana gently touched his arm, her glance taking in Rowan as her cheeks grew pink. "Have no worries, Thomas," she said in a near whisper.

The priest's brow furrowed in confusion, but Thomas felt certain that he understood what she was telling him. He gave her a tender nod of approval, of thanks. Rowan was right, he was indeed lucky to be marrying such a woman.

"I will," he boldly stated.

After that, Gloriana went through her responses to the challenge questions, not even hesitating, although he had held his breath in anticipation of her refusing him. When the ordeal was finally over, he smiled. His smile was so big in his relief that his cheeks actually ached from the strangeness of it.

She blinked at him in surprise, and then gave him a tentative smile in return.

***

"Tis time, my lady," Thomas said as he put a hand to Gloriana's back and nudged her away from where she'd stood watching the people celebrate their marriage.

"As you wish." She spoke the words quietly, hoping he didn't hear the anxiety she felt. Her heart raced at his touch, at the deep timbre of his voice. She'd spent last night replaying what she'd seen in the solar, how she'd felt about it, more curious than anything else.

"Do not fear me, little one."

She noticed that his expression was earnest. His eyes darkened with heat. *Desire? For her?* She'd worried that if he had such strong feelings—as was obvious—for a man, in particular Rowan, could he have any for a woman, for her? Clearly, he could. She liked that idea. Yet she was reluctant to go upstairs to their bedchamber with him. She stopped him at the foot of the stairs and looked up at him, her stomach clenching. "Tis not you specifically I fear." She couldn't meet his eyes. "Tis the marriage bed." She swallowed hard, fighting back tears of shame. "Tis failing as a wife. Again."

He cursed, drawing the attention of a handful of people nearby. One of them Gerald.

Gerald immediately approached them, back rigid, determination etched on his time-lined face. "Have you need of me, my lady?"

She watched the two men share a look of frustration. Gerald's brow was furrowed, his eyes squinted tight. She knew he would defend her to the death and, in spite of knowing Thomas's reputation as a good and fair leader of men, he didn't trust the younger man yet. And Thomas's expression was tense, his jaw clenched, his posture stiff. He didn't like being challenged.

When Thomas would have bit out a response, Gloriana forced a smile and shook her head. "All is fine, Sir Gerald." She didn't want the two important men in her life to come to blows. She had caused the problem. She needed to stop fearing a man who didn't deserve it. "Do not worry," she added and forced her nerves under control.

Gerald appeared to calm down at her insistence. But Thomas remained rigid and said grimly, "I am *not* Geoffrey Stewart. Your lady will never suffer at my hands."

Gerald nodded acceptance before moving away, but Gloriana sensed there was an underlying message to Thomas that he would hold her new husband to what he'd said.

"Tis the truth, Gloriana. I will never harm you." He touched the side of her face, thumbed at a tear that had trickled down her cheek. "And you will not fail me as a wife. Nor do I believe you failed Stewart."

"But..." She started to protest, thinking of the many times Geoffrey had tried to have sex with her and hadn't been able to get his cock hard enough to thrust it into her. He'd been furious, blamed her. She'd suffered dearly for the failures each time.

Thomas leaned down, cupped her face, and kissed her. She was so surprised that she sucked in a breath. He hadn't smashed his lips into hers. It didn't cause her pain. No, his lips settled quite nicely against hers. And then she felt his tongue sliding along her lips until they parted almost of their own accord. His tongue eased into her mouth, dancing lightly against hers. Her entire body tingled, yearned for more. She felt the hardness of the ridge of his cock beneath his braies as he pressed against her. Her pulse raced.

After a minute, he eased back and she heard him laugh. It was a rusty sound, as if he hadn't laughed in a very long time and was out of practice. She blinked at him, a bit irritated. "Did I do something wrong?" To her shock, he laughed again and then scooped her into his arms. "Nay, wife, you did nothing wrong. Your innocence surprises me, amuses me, and draws me."

She squirmed in his arms and nearly made them both fall as he started up the stairs. "I'm *not* innocent!"

He continued moving upward. "After your reaction to that kiss, I've a feeling you're nearly as innocent as a virgin bride. I'm quite pleased with that."

The kiss had been something new to her; Geoffrey's kisses had never been pleasurable. They'd only caused her pain, and led to even more pain. Yet she found herself looking up at Thomas's full lips and remembering how they'd felt against hers. Heat curled through her. She really wanted to ask him to do it again.

"I'm not a virgin," she said instead, beginning to worry a bit about going to bed with him. She thought about the great length of him that she'd seen and that she'd felt pressed against her. "What if I can't..."

They were almost to the bedchamber now and he stopped to look down at her. "What if you can't what?"

Her face felt hot, and she glanced quickly down his body and up again. "What if *that* doesn't fit inside me? It seemed awfully big."

His chest appeared to puff out. "I appreciate the compliment, my lady, but you need not worry."

"I am worried, though."

"Believe me, every inch will fit inside you. And you will enjoy it."

She wasn't so sure about enjoying it. "I did not enjoy it when Geoffrey..." She didn't finish the thought, embarrassed, ashamed.

He set her down, pulled her to him, and kissed her so hard, so passionately that she was lost in a whirlwind of sensations.

Then he eased away and looked serious. "After tonight, I can promise you that you will no longer even think about Stewart. I have much to teach you about how exquisite the sex act can be."

When she continued to look doubtful, he sighed. "All I ask, Gloriana, is that you trust in me."

She let him nudge her into their bedchamber, but her legs turned wobbly. Her gaze landed on the bed, with the fur and linens already turned down. Her heart pounded as horrible memories raced through her mind. She thought again of how big Thomas was, everywhere. Panic made her breaths come in short spurts, her hands twisted anxiously at the sides of her gown. Staring at the bed, a sickening wave of terror swelled within her.

*No! She couldn't do this! What if...* Her vision blurred and she swayed. "I can't..." and then she crumpled to the floor.

## Chapter Three

Turning, Thomas closed and locked the chamber's door. He heard an odd rustling sound followed by a thump. The long-time warrior in him immediately reached for a weapon he wasn't carrying. His first thought was that someone had hidden in their room and stepped out to attack them. When he spun around, he found his new wife lying unconscious on the hard stone floor. *What could have caused this?*

His gaze darted around the chamber even as his heart pounded. He would kill with his bare hands anyone who had dared to harm her.

He hurried toward her and swept his gaze again around the room. *No one.* They were alone. The knowledge didn't lessen his fear for her. "Gloriana!" He bent over her to gently touch her face with a shaking hand. Already he could see a sizable lump forming on the side of her forehead. She looked so pale, so still. *Too still.* Yet he saw the weak rise and fall of her chest. He ever so carefully stroked her cheek again.

"Gloriana," he coaxed, but received no response.

Heart pounding in worry, he climbed to his feet. *Help.* He needed to get help. The desperate words rolled over and over in his mind as he strode back to the door and impatiently unlocked it, jerked it open.

With a last glance at Gloriana's still form, he raced down the hallway toward the stairs, yelling, "Rowan! Gerald! Someone find Marie! Gloriana has been hurt!"

Immediately the happy raised voices in the great hall quieted. Tension replaced the celebration. He yelled once more, "Rowan! Gerald! Marie!"

He didn't wait a second more, ignoring the questions shot back at him. As he sped back to the chamber, he barely noted footsteps hurrying toward him. His heart raced. He could not lose her! He could not! *He would not!*

Tearing back into the chamber, he realized she hadn't moved at all. Panic curled deeper into him. He threw himself down on his knees next to her and patted her face once more. "Gloriana. Dear God, Gloriana, wake up," he begged, hearing the husky fear in his voice.

"What have you done?" Gerald questioned in a growl. His eyes were cold, hard when he stormed next to Thomas and shoved him away. "I'll kill you for this!"

Thomas lunged to his feet and shoved him back. "I did nothing," he roared. He bunched his fists, prepared to defend himself with blows if it was necessary. "I am not responsible for this."

But Gerald looked down at Gloriana and fury sparked in his narrowed eyes. "She did not want this marriage. She feared it. And now..."

He lunged for Thomas, his muscled arms outstretched and reaching for Thomas's throat.

Thomas shifted to the side enough that he took charge. He didn't want to fight with this man he knew was only concerned for his lady, defending her as a warrior would when he had no weapons on him. He grabbed hold of Gerald's arm and held tight. "I. Did. Not. Do. This," he gritted out.

Rowan tore into the room and wedged between them. He shoved them apart, causing Thomas to stagger back at the same time Gerald did. The soldiers who had rushed in behind Rowan caught the older man, and Thomas breathed a sigh of relief. Gerald seemed to calm down, yet wariness remained in his eyes.

Now that the situation was diffused, Thomas returned his focus to Gloriana. She was still not moving. His heart hammered in worry and he moved next to his wife.

Rowan stepped to Thomas's side. "What happened?" he asked in a voice echoing his concern.

Before he could answer, Thomas watched Marie jostle her way into the room. She wiggled her way through the men who dwarfed her, all looking worriedly down at their lady.

Marie looked pointedly at him and repeated Rowan's question, "What happened?"

He didn't want to answer questions. He wanted someone to help his wife. Yet he called on his fading patience and said, "I don't know. I turned to close the door, then I heard a sound." He thought about his moment of panic, his need to defend his wife if necessary. His palms were sweating and his patience almost gone.

"I thought someone had waited in here to attack us. I had no weapon.

I…" He blew out a frustrated breath. "I turned around and found Gloriana on the floor."

Marie knelt beside his wife and gently examined the bump on Gloriana's head. "My poor sweet lady," she crooned.

"She was terrified of you bedding her," Gerald snapped in disgust. "She didn't want this marriage. Not after…"

Thomas looked over his shoulder at the angry, distraught man. Although disliking the comments, he understood them. He might not know exactly what had gone on between Gloriana and Stewart, but he sensed enough to be sickened by it. And he admired the way her bailiff was determined to stand by her now. Still, he had to defend himself. "She didn't appear terrified when I kissed her. She never once told me she didn't want this marriage."

Gerald snorted, his face growing nearly as red as his hair. "There was nothing she could do about it. The King decreed you were to take her for a wife. She could not refuse."

"Enough!" Rowan snarled. "This is your new lord you are speaking to. He is *nothing* like Stewart. You would be wise to understand that now."

The tension was thick in the room. Thomas watched Rowan and Gerald glare in challenge at each other; tempers were on edge. All here were worried about the beauty lying at their feet. Thomas especially.

And then a small, quiet moan drew everyone's attention.

"She awakens, my lord," Marie stated abruptly, relief in her tone.

Thomas forgot everyone else and focused solely on his wife. His pulse hammered at how pale she seemed, how fragile. Gloriana's eyelids fluttered open and then closed as she winced and reached to touch her head. Tears misted his eyes, a lump formed in his throat. He barely knew this woman he'd just married. Yet he was drawn to her for far more than her beauty. He wanted time, years, to learn all of her secrets, to release the passion he sensed laying guarded inside her. He did not want her to be scared of him.

With all of those thoughts tumbling around in him, he leaned over her and tried to look comforting. His hand shook as he smoothed a strand of hair from her pale, strained face. He didn't care who saw that small weakness in him. "Are you all right?" She shifted to stretch out her bent legs, groaning. "My head hurts." Pain pinched her face and she noticed the people gazing down at her. "Why am I on the floor?" She looked up at him in confusion.

"You fainted, for some reason." He stroked her cheek, unable to keep from touching her in some way. He drew in a steadying breath and scowled out of worry. "You will *not* do this again. Do you hear me? You will *not* frighten me like this again." He knew how ridiculous that sounded, but the words had tumbled out.

Rowan's hand settled on his shoulder and Thomas drew comfort by the touch. It helped settle his nerves.

"I doubt she planned this simply to annoy you, my lord," Rowan said with amusement lacing his tone. Thomas suspected he made the comment to further ease his fears.

Gloriana huffed. "You cannot order me not to faint, husband." Then her face softened and she studied his expression. She asked in surprise, "You were frightened? Because of me?"

He decided he'd appeared weak enough in front of his men. He chose not to answer, although he gave her a slight nod. Then he shifted so he could scoop her from the floor. But, because of the awkward way in which she lay and having both Rowan and Marie standing so close, lifting her was difficult. Once he had her in his arms and was on his feet, he frowned down at her. "Mayhap you should eat less bread in the morn." She gasped in shock. Marie giggled. And Rowan chuckled.

Thomas carried her toward the bed, wondering what insanity had taken over his mind to say such a thing.

She narrowed her eyes at him. "Mayhap I should have married a man not so feeble." She glanced around him, smiling devilishly. "A well-muscled, hearty man like Sir Rowan."

Now he did growl. "I'm just as muscled, if not more so." He lay her down a little less gently than he should have on the bed.

She hissed in reaction and squeezed her eyes shut in pain.

He immediately regretted letting his temper get the best of him even for a mere second. "I'm sorry, wife. Forgive me."

"I shouldn't have teased you." Suddenly she grabbed at her stomach and shot up in bed. "I'm going to be sick!"

Marie must have anticipated this for she pushed him aside to thrust a chamber pot in front of Gloriana. "You will be fine, my lady."

Thomas watched helplessly as his young wife retched into the pot. Behind him he heard the other men quickly leaving the room, apparently relieved she would be okay and preferring not to witness her heaving up what little she'd eaten at the wedding feast. But he would not leave her side, even if observing her made his stomach feel queasy. Rowan had not left the room and moved around him. He stood next to the bed to carefully smooth Gloriana's hair back as she retched a final time. He glanced back at Thomas, his eyes worried, but his tone was reassuring. "She'll be all right. I've had such a head wound myself."

He held her long hair to the side as she gingerly lay back. "Her head will be wickedly sore for a few days. She'll probably be rather dazed for the rest of today and want to sleep a lot." He eased away from the bed and let Marie wipe Gloriana's face with a cloth she'd soaked in a basin of water on the nearby trunk. "You should watch over her. She needs rest, but awaken her every couple of hours."

Thomas studied his friend and recognized nearly the same worry in his expression that Thomas felt. He'd witnessed the tender way he'd touched her hair. Rowan, too, was developing strong feelings for this woman. If Thomas hadn't been ordered to marry her, would Rowan have pursued her? He preferred making love to men, to him in particular… or so Rowan had told him. But he occasionally had sex with women, including Marie, who now watched them both curiously. Yet Gloriana seemed to have captured his attention, and Thomas had seen the way she looked at Rowan at times. He should feel jealous, and he did, but only slightly. He'd felt her response, her desire for him, when he'd kissed her. They were all three in a difficult situation. He loved Rowan, needed him. And he felt the beginnings of tenderness for Gloriana.

"I'd like to get out of this gown," Gloriana said weakly, snaring his attention once more.

Marie instantly said, "I'll help you." Then she handed Thomas the chamber pot and smiled in mischief at him. "Mayhap you can see to this while I attend your wife."

***

By the time both Rowan and Thomas had left the chamber and Marie finished undressing her, Gloriana was exhausted and mortified. Lying naked beneath the linen, she patiently waited for Marie to bring her a fresh chemise. Instead her friend headed for the door.

In a panic, Gloriana called out, "My chemise."

Marie simply stopped at the door and smiled. "Tis your wedding day, my lady." "But…" *Dear Lord!* Now Gloriana remembered the thoughts that had gone through her mind before she'd apparently fainted. "But Thomas… he's so… so big!"

Marie gave a lilting laugh and her eyes danced with amusement, envy, too. "Aye, he's a brawny man, your husband." She giggled. "I'm suspecting he's big in *many* ways. You lucky woman."

Gloriana knew for a fact just how big Thomas was in the particular way she sensed her friend was talking about. It still amazed her that Rowan had been able to… *No!* She shouldn't be thinking of what she'd witnessed. It wasn't her business. Well, maybe it was in a way. *No!* That was between her husband and his first knight.

Evidently Marie saw something in her expression that caused her concern for she stopped smiling. She said gently, "He's nothing like Geoffrey. You can see it in Lord Thomas's eyes, especially when he looks at you. You should trust him. Give him a chance."

Gloriana forced aside the other thoughts. She remembered what Thomas had said to her as they entered the bedchamber, when she'd first started to panic. "Tis what he told me," she said in a whisper. "I just…I don't know if I can."

"You can," Marie stated at the same time Thomas stepped into the doorway beside her and said the same words.

He looked down at Marie. "You can leave us now. Your lady will be safe in my hands."

With a smile of encouragement, Marie walked by him, but not away until she boldly said, "Be gentle with her, my lord. She's known far too little of such treatment." Her heart beating wildly, Gloriana watched Thomas close and lock the door. He was such a large man. His broad shoulders stretched the fabric of his tunic. His legs were long and muscled as well, and his arms bulged with the strength to wave a broadsword with little effort. He could crush her with no trouble at all. Yet instinctively she didn't fear him in that way. When he faced her, he frowned. "I will never use my size against you, little one. Nor my strength." "Stop calling me 'little one.'" She saw amusement flicker in his eyes and wondered if he hadn't used the term to irritate her, to refocus her thoughts. "Never mistake me for being weak because of my size."

He cocked an eyebrow and walked closer. "Yet you fainted at the thought of my bedding you? At the knowledge that I'm far bigger than you?"

"Wedding nerves," she protested, not wanting to admit he was probably right. He kept walking closer. The room seemed to shrink, making her tense. She put a hand to her throbbing head. "I'm tired, hurting." The wretched, stubborn man didn't stop moving. He stared down at her and calmly pulled his tunic off. She gaped at the hard chest, at the sinewy muscles, at the light spattering of dark hair. Then she saw the jagged scar across his lower abdomen and glanced up at the one on his face. He'd been seriously hurt at some point. Her tender woman's heart ached for him.

He must have seen the concern on her face, the wetness in her eyes. He froze, blinking. "These happened long ago. I'm far more careful now when I battle."

"I do not like warring, or the thought of you going off to do so again." She bit her lower lip, puzzled why she'd said such a thing. Warring was what men like him did. She knew well of his reputation, that he was a favored knight of Edward's. As was Rowan; another realization that she didn't want to think about.

He toed off his low boots. "Nor do I like battling." He looked at her intently. "There was a time in my life when I wanted no more than to battle. I had much anger in me. I could not stay in one place, make peace with anything." Her breath hitched when he put a hand to his braies.

"And now?" she questioned uncertainly. "Now I'm weary of so much traveling, so much battling, and so much death." He started to lower his braies, hesitated. "I have a new holding and have told the King I wish to train soldiers rather than be one. He will allow that…for now."

She couldn't take her gaze away from where his hand held the braies low on his body, from where she saw the fullness of his large cock only partially hidden from her sight. She swallowed hard. She didn't want to see all of him, and yet she was anxious to see all of him.

The braies went down another inch. "I have a son." He frowned at that. "The boy, James, hardly knows me. I want him with me."

"How…how old is he?" Her heart raced in anticipation of when he finally dropped his braies.

"Nearly ten by now. He has lived his entire life with my sister Elizabeth and her husband, Lord Abernon." His expression hardened. "Abernon does not approve of me. He will not give up my son easily."

The pain in his tone snared her attention. "But James is *your* son. He cannot keep him from you."

He studied her warily. "You would not mind my son coming here? You would act his stepmother, if he allowed it?"

There was such a vulnerable look in his eyes that it touched her heart. "I've long wanted a child. I would gladly act as his stepmother."

Eager anticipation warred with concern within her. Would his son accept her? She was generally good with children, but this boy had clearly already had much to deal with. Could she reach him, make him trust in the love she would give him? For she knew it wouldn't take much for her to give her heart to the boy.

"Aye, I would treat him as my own." While she watched Thomas's relief settle in his eyes, she drew on her courage. She raised her chin and held her breath as she said, "I want a child of my body as well. That is all I ask of you in this marriage. Give me a babe to love."

He stiffened and his eyes flared with grimness. "Although it could happen, this is *not* something I want. I do not wish you to become pregnant."

Her hopes and dreams shattered. Her heart sank. She couldn't seem to draw in a breath. Everything in her hurt, worse than her head. She didn't know if she could even have children, since Geoffrey hadn't been able to get her with child. But she desperately wanted one. Watching the mothers with their children around the castle had long been difficult. The smiles and laughter and hugs they shared, especially mothers with their really young children. She had longed for such things for what felt like forever. She'd ached to hold a small, warm babe in her arms. She'd thought she had accepted that she'd never have those experiences when Geoffrey had been her husband. But Thomas was a different man. She'd had such hope, but now… His words had cut deep. She fought the urge to cry out her pain.

Trembling in disappointment, she barely noticed the tears trickling down her cheeks. She couldn't give up so easily. She looked at Thomas and begged in a near whisper, "I will care for the baby myself. You won't have to do anything, other than to give me one. I promise."

She held her breath, praying he would change his mind. He didn't. She watched his face harden and saw determination flare in his expressive eyes. "You will *not* become pregnant."

With that, he pulled up his braies, jerked on his tunic, and stomped back into his boots. He strode from the room, slamming the door behind him. It felt like he'd struck her. She reeled and curled into herself. How could Thomas have told her he would be gentle with her, be far different than Geoffrey with her? In a way his heartless denial of the only thing she wanted in the world was much worse. She'd been a fool to think her life might be better with him. A fool to dare to hope again.

***

Thomas strode through the great hall, shoving past anyone who tried to stop him. Every eye was focused on him as he sped through the keep's door. Rage made him ignore everyone; made him determined only to reach the stables and find his horse. He needed to ride, hard. He needed to get control of his anger. He wasn't angry at Gloriana; no, he was upset with himself. It wasn't her fault he couldn't give her a baby like she wanted. It was fear, gut deep fear, of having her die in childbirth that tortured him. He should have explained to her rather than snarling at her.

His hands fisted at his sides. He ground his jaw tightly. He shouldn't have reacted like that; he should have had more control. She'd suffered a fall, gotten hurt, and now he'd hurt her more. Disgust filled him. Later he would try to explain his feelings to her. For now he needed distance.

***

Rowan heard the sudden silence around him as he was flirting with Marie. He turned in time to see Thomas storming down the stairs, his expression furious. He didn't know what the hell could have happened between him and Gloriana, but he knew that it must be something serious. And he knew his friend needed him, even if he hadn't asked for his help.

He nudged Marie toward the stairs. "Go see to your lady. I fear our lord has said something that he will later regret. He said something that has caused him to seek time alone to settle his temper." To his relief, she hurried to obey him.

When he looked up again, he found Gerald heading for the keep's door, along with several other frowning men. Rowan rushed to catch them. He stepped into the doorway just ahead of them, blocking their way, and shaking his head. "No. Do not go after him. Leave this to me."

"If he has done something to hurt…" Gerald said in a fierce growl, but stopped at Rowan's equally severe scowl.

"Your lord would never physically hurt a woman. Never." He blew out a breath. "But he may have said something he shouldn't have. It will eat at him. He will make amends later, but for now he needs to get away and calm down."

Rowan rubbed a hand through his hair, pinching his lips together in frustration. "The man knows how to make war, but he struggles with showing a gentle side. You'll have to give him time to adjust. All of this is a big change for him."

Gerald didn't look particularly appeased, but he gave a curt nod.

By the time Rowan made it to the bailey, he saw Thomas riding across the drawbridge. The guards at the gate and on the parapet looked down at him in concern. "Do not worry. I will go after him." He heard another soldier coming up behind him, clearly intending to go with him. He faced the other man. "I will go alone. Tis best. I will bring your lord back later."

***

Thomas rode like the demons of Hell were after him. He drove his powerful destrier as hard as he'd ever driven him. By the time he regained some control over his anger and reined in, they were miles from the castle and the village. Lather coated his horse's back and the big black stallion's sides heaved as he drew in breaths. Guilt for abusing the loyal beast tore at him. Even more guilt weighed heavily on him for the way he'd treated Gloriana.

He slid from the bare back and stood staring from the edge of the forest at the lake to which he'd ridden. His own breaths came hard. He shuddered from the intensity of his emotions and from the wild ride. It would be difficult to go back and face the people he'd stormed past, even harder to make peace with Gloriana, if that were even possible. He stared at the lake and waited. Rowan was not far behind him. He'd known in his gut that his first, his lover would come after him, and he'd heard the other horse pounding closer and closer. Yet Rowan had given him time to settle a bit before he caught up with him. A wise man.

"What eats at you, my friend?" Rowan rode up beside him and slipped from his horse.

Thomas noted that Rowan hadn't taken the time to saddle his horse, but then neither had he. An urgent need to get away had been Thomas's reasoning. An equally powerful desire to come after him had no doubt been Rowan's excuse. Thomas would not have welcomed any other man right now. But he needed Rowan. Desperately needed him. "She wants a baby," he said simply.

Rowan nodded. He knew Thomas's fears, knew the reasons for them. Still, he said, "She is young. Most women do want children." He hesitated. "Although I don't know why she and Stewart didn't have one by now. Mayhap…"

"Mayhap she can't bear a child. Mayhap he couldn't give her one," Thomas interrupted and kicked at a twig. A breeze fluttered over him, but it did nothing to settle his frustration. "But mayhap *I* can give her one. Except I *cannot.* You know I *cannot.*"

Rowan glanced at the horses standing nearby as they'd been trained. He looked toward the lake, large and blue, blue as the clear sky overhead. Something rustled in the bushes. Thomas grew impatient watching the other man, waiting for him to speak.

"I told her I refuse to get her pregnant. She pleaded with me, but I did not give in. Not even when I heard her crying as I stormed from the room." Her crying had made him feel worse, made him ride his horse even harder. "She didn't deserve to be treated that way. Especially when she already fears you, worries about having you take her to bed." Rowan sounded angry on her behalf.

Thomas didn't like being reminded of her fearing him. It would only be worse now that he'd flashed his temper at her. He thought about Rowan's words, about the way he'd seen his friend looking at her. "You are attracted to Gloriana, aren't you?" Rowan tensed and then shrugged. "She is a beautiful woman."

"*Marie* is a beautiful woman."

"And a generous woman in bed. But..." Rowan shrugged again. "But, yes, I find Gloriana appealing."

Rowan blew out a deep breath. "It will *not* become a problem for us. I would never act on my sexual attraction to her. I would never hurt you in that way. Or her." Thomas wasn't so sure Rowan would be able to keep his word on that, not if he was drawn to her as much as Thomas believed. He would think more on the matter at another time. Right now he needed... As if reading his thoughts, Rowan snapped, "You need to pay for hurting Gloriana. Pay for letting your temper get the best of you." He pointed into the thin patch of pines nearby. "Go and brace yourself on the tree stump there."

Thomas didn't move. "I may deserve a sound thrashing with a switch, but I will not allow it."

"Tempting as that sounds, it is not what I have in mind." Rowan cupped the clear evidence of his hardened cock. "I will fuck you mercilessly. You will have difficulty riding back by the time I'm finished with you. That should be punishment enough."

Punishment or not, a shudder of anticipation swept through Thomas and he walked quickly away. He already had his braies lowered to his ankles and stood with hands braced against the stump by the time Rowan came up behind him. Even with the scent of pines around him, he could smell the scent of his lover's arousal. His cock hardened at once.

Rowan came up directly behind him. Thomas tensed, tightening his bare buttocks as Rowan put a callused hand on them. He tried to relax when Rowan pressed his long shaft against Thomas's crack and rubbed. As Thomas moaned, Rowan reached around and grabbed his cock. He sucked in a breath, then gasped, "Yes."

His friend was in total control, and he savored the feeling. There were times, like now, when he needed someone else to be the strong one. He closed his eyes and let Rowan stroke his cock. It felt so good. Too good. He needed Rowan to drive into him, punish him for the way he'd hurt Gloriana. "Now. I need you now!"

But Rowan was in charge, and he was making Thomas pay in his own way, in his own time. Thomas panted and moaned while Rowan continued pumping his shaft. Finally Rowan had mercy on him and brought him to release. Cum shot from Thomas's cock, enough that Rowan could coat his rod and focus his attention behind Thomas.

Thomas was recovering, yet he desperately needed more. "Fuck me!" he gritted out, already half-crazy in anticipation. "Now! Fuck me now!"

Rowan gripped his hips and put the head of his cock to Thomas's tight passage. Thomas tensed, anxious, ready. Behind him, his lover said grimly, "No preparation this time. You don't deserve it."

Thomas held fast to the stump, braced for the hard thrust to come. "No, I don't deserve it. Do it!"

The sharp thrust drove Rowan's thick rod deep into his ass. Without any preparation, it hurt. He cursed and forced himself to endure the immediate burning of his stretched hole. But Rowan had the courtesy to hold still for a second to let Thomas adjust as best he could.

"Ready for a hard ride?" Rowan asked as he tightened his grip on Thomas's hips. Ready or not, he was going to get it. Thomas lowered his head and braced his arms again. He focused on the ground, on the sounds around him, not on the punishment his ass was about to take from the large cock stuffed deep inside it. "Yes."

Rowan began moving, thrusting deep, pulling nearly out and ramming even deeper again. He groaned with effort, never letting loose of Thomas's hips. Never slowing the steady invasion.

Thomas grunted from the intensity of being taken so determinedly. It felt incredible as always. Yet it hurt, too. There was no chance to recover, no chance to enjoy the fierce drives. It was not about mutual pleasure this time. This was about paying for his cruelty to Gloriana. Rowan had been right, by the time he was finished with his ass, Thomas would have a hard time riding back to Middlemound.

Finally Rowan stiffened, then drove deep and fast three more times. He roared out as hot cum flooded Thomas's passage. Then he stood behind Thomas for a couple of minutes still locked deep inside him, and they both regained their breath.

"Better now?" Rowan asked as he pulled out of Thomas's ass.

Thomas remained bent over another few seconds, adjusting to the sudden emptiness. He still burned. Before he stood, he picked up some leaves off the ground. He wiped the juices dripping out of him and tossed the leaves aside.

Turning, he pulled up his braies and met Rowan's concerned gaze. "My ass is sore as hell, but, yes, I'm better."

Both of them went to their horses. Thomas groaned and shifted uncomfortably as he mounted. "Yes, sore as hell."

***

It was dark and the keep was silent by the time Thomas crept into their bedchamber. Gloriana had waited all afternoon and evening for his return. She'd cried so many tears there weren't any left inside her. Marie had tried to comfort her, but she hadn't wanted to tell her friend the cruel things Thomas had said to her. As ridiculous as it was, she still held to a faint hope that she could change his mind. But first she would have to ask him why he felt so strongly opposed to having another child. Maybe it was just that he saw her as too fragile.

A sound on the stairway seemed to echo loudly and drew her attention. She held her breath, sensing it was Thomas...at last. Her heart raced as she heard footsteps growing closer, then the handle on the door rattled before he pushed it open with a whisper of noise. As the door closed again, she stiffened. Should she let him think she was asleep? Should she confront him?

She pulled on her courage and opened her eyes to face the man who had crushed her feelings earlier.

She'd left the bedside candles burning, and she saw the uncertainty and wariness in his expression when he turned in her direction. When he realized she was staring at him, he started. Had he hoped she would be asleep? At the same time, she wondered why he hadn't slept in another chamber tonight.

"Are you all right?" She hadn't meant to speak first, but the slump to his shoulders worried her.

He stood stiffly just inside the chamber. "Tis I who should be asking that question." She scooted up in bed to lean against the headboard. She wore a chemise now, having decided he must not even intend to bed her if he didn't want to get her with child. His assurances that he would fit inside her seemed like so long ago. Unimportant now. "My head still throbs now and again." It was her heart that hurt the most. If anything, his shoulders appeared to slump even more. "I've caused you nothing but pain, and I do regret it." He turned to leave.

"Where are you going?" she asked and he stilled.

"I can't imagine that you want me in your bed this night."

She studied him as best she could in the dim light. He looked weary to the bone. Fool that she was, she motioned him closer. "You don't appear up to ravishing me, so you are welcome to share our bed."

He blinked in surprise, but took another few seconds before walking across the room. "No, there'll be no ravishing you this night." "Good. Now come to bed, my lord. I'm quite tired myself." She settled back under the linen covering, squirming to pull her chemise down as it had ridden up her legs.

For the second time that day, he pulled his tunic off in front of her. And, again, she felt her heart flutter at the sight of his powerful body. Then he toed off his boots and pushed them away.

When his hands moved to lower his braies, he stopped to look at her in concern. "I sleep naked, but mayhap this time…"

She had been watching him closely, not meaning to, but unable to stop herself. Before she could mind her tongue, she said, "Tis all right, Thomas. I am clothed." Resignation passed over his beard stubbled face. After another second, he removed his braies. His cock wasn't as long and hard as she'd seen it with Rowan, and as she'd expected to see it earlier. Oddly, she felt disappointed.

She tried to close her eyes, to not watch him further, as he sat on the side of the bed. But his quiet moan drew her attention once more. "Husband?" she asked in concern.

He avoided looking directly at her and stretched out beside her, on top of the linens. "I'm fine. Just a bit sore from riding so hard today."

He shifted again, gave another quiet moan. This time she turned toward him. "Is there something I can do? Some salve I can apply?" The thought of touching him in any manner sent shivers through her. Yet she didn't want him to suffer, even if he'd made her suffer.

But he was already half asleep. He mumbled, "Tis Rowan's fault. He rode me too hard."

"What?" She didn't understand. Rowan had returned much earlier and had come to check on her. He'd told her that he'd caught up with Thomas. They'd talked, he'd said. But he hadn't looked her in the eye, either. She nibbled on the corner of her lower lip, pondering Rowan's odd reaction. She studied Thomas more closely. Something was odd, something that niggled at her curious nature.

She lightly touched Thomas's face to capture his attention. He looked wearily at her. "Did you and Rowan…" Her face flamed, but she pressed on, "Did you suck cock? Like I… like I saw yesterday."

"Good God!" He sat bolt upright in bed, his eyes wide in shock. He also winced and quickly lay back down. "No, we did not 'suck cock' as you so delicately put it."

But she knew there was more to what had happened between he and Rowan today. Something that had to do with his obvious discomfort. "Then what do you mean 'he rode me too hard'?"

"God's teeth! Did I actually say that?" He sounded distressed, worried.

She nodded. "Aye, but you were partially asleep." She sat up and looked down at him, determined to get an answer. "What did you mean?"

He was silent for several minutes, his face contorted in deep thought. Finally he heaved a heavy sigh and met her gaze. "You already know that Rowan and I…" He struggled with what to say. "That we…"

Gloriana was getting impatient. "Aye. You have relations, of a sort. It does not bother me." She pinned him with a prodding gaze. "Explain about this business of 'riding you too hard.'"

He squeezed his eyes shut, muttered something, and then faced her again. "We sometimes do far more than you witnessed."

"Far more?" She cocked her head and studied him. She still thought about how she'd observed the two powerful men engaged in a sexual act that she'd previously found appalling. At least it had been with Geoffrey. Did Thomas mean that he, too, sucked on Rowan's shaft? What else could two men do together?

She furrowed her brow trying to figure it out. When she couldn't, she asked, "I cannot understand this *riding* matter. Nor this *far more* issue." She found that she was intrigued by whatever happened intimately between Thomas and Rowan.

"I really don't want to discuss this, Gloriana." He tried to roll to his other side, but gave a quiet hiss as he moved.

She pulled him to his back once more, frowning at the flinch of pain that crossed his face. "I will tell no one, my lord, I promise. But I wish to understand. Especially when I see that you are in obvious discomfort."

He clenched his jaw and appeared to gnash his teeth before he bit out, "We fuck. All right? This time he fucked me. Hard."

She reeled in astonishment, blinking in confusion. "You mean he…" She gaped at him and then glanced toward his slowly growing cock. "You mean he put his rod inside you? But I don't understand. How can that be?" She truly couldn't imagine how such a thing was possible.

His patience had clearly reached an end. He rolled to his side again and pointed to his butt crack. "He drove his rod into my ass. Fast. Hard. Mercilessly." He glanced at her over his shoulder with a sour expression. "Are you satisfied now?"

Instead of being satisfied, she was more curious, worried as well. Before he could resist, she pushed him to his stomach and gently parted his butt cheeks.

He tried to bat her hands away. "What are you doing, woman? Stop it!"

She ignored him and studied his ass. In truth, it was a very nice ass, firm. Unlike hers, which was far too flabby, in her opinion. Her face heated at such thoughts. "It looks very sore, husband."

She promptly climbed off the bed and hurried to the trunk where she kept herbs and salves.

"Now what are you doing? Come back to bed."

She planted her hands on her hips and snapped, "You need something to soothe the pain."

"Good God, Gloriana! You are *not* going to apply one of your healing salves to my ass. Forget it. I'll be fine on the morrow."

He got up, scooped her into his arms, and lay her on the bed. Then he stretched out on his stomach once more, growling, "Go. To. Sleep."

"I only want to help." She gently touched his buttocks.

"Leave my ass alone." He pushed her hand away and planted his pillow over his bottom.

She huffed at his impossible attitude. Fine, if he wanted to suffer needlessly tonight, he could. But she'd check on his ass on the morrow. If it wasn't better by then, she'd apply her salve no matter how much he grouched about it.

## Chapter Four

"I need to talk to you," Thomas said, walking to where Rowan was practice training in the bailey. When his friend raised an eyebrow in question, he blew out a breath of frustration. "Now. I need to talk to you now."

"Another matter of some urgency? Something you'll share with me this time?" Rowan nodded at the soldier he'd been sword sparring with. "Remember to keep your shield up higher."

Thomas knew his first knight was testy because he hadn't been included when Thomas had talked to Middlemound's baliff earlier and had sent the man and eleven others off on a task for him. "I merely sent Gerald and the others to deliver a message to Elizabeth at Abernon."

Rowan walked beside him as Thomas headed for the paddocks, wanting to talk somewhere at least partially private. "Am I your *first* knight here or not?"

"Of course you are." Thomas understood his friend's anger. As the first knight, he should issue the orders for the other men, or at least know about them before Thomas gave them. "You were busy with other duties and I wanted to get the men on their way. I wasn't thinking clearly."

They stopped to lean against the first paddock's fencing, and Thomas blew out a frustrated breath. "I've been distracted since yesterday. You. James. Gloriana."

"I know you want to bring your son here. I'm just not sure the timing is right." Rowan glanced at him, clearly already forgiving him for giving the order to the men. "Shouldn't you get more settled here first? Particularly with Gloriana."

Thomas frowned, thinking about his sister and her husband. "Abernon is going to fight letting my son come here, so I thought I'd get the negotiations started now."

"You're most likely right. James has been in his household almost since birth. Abernon would see him as his son by now, more than yours." He met Thomas's gaze. "I fear, too, that James will not want to leave the home he knows."

"I have much to battle here, this I know. But I want my son with me." Thomas well knew this could be the hardest battle he'd ever fought. Abernon was a good man, his people were loyal to him. He'd earned the respect of their King and many nobles throughout England. His opinion of Thomas was low, except as a warrior. It irritated him that he would have to prove his worth as a father to his own son, but he would. Somehow. Hopefully having Gloriana at his side and supporting him in this would help. "I *will* have my way in this matter."

"You know I will assist you in any way necessary."

Thomas nodded. They would each go through Hell itself if necessary for the other. That had been proven time and again as they'd fought side-by-side in Tunis; protected each other's backs, and tended each other's wounds.

"My part in your distractions?" Rowan lowered his voice; glancing cautiously around to be sure they were still alone. "Are you upset with how I handled you yesterday? Even though you did deserve it."

His ass still hurt, but Thomas shook his head. "The pounding was deserved, as you said. I'll recover." He closed his eyes for a second and thought about last night. "Gloriana wanted to help me." He blew out a heavy breath, hesitating before he added, "She wanted to put some of her healing salve on my ass."

Rowan straightened and looked directly at him, amusement dancing in his eyes. "What did you say?"

Remembering how his wife had gently touched him and then became bolder, he, too, looked around to be sure they were alone. Thomas said stiffly, "She kept pressing me about you and me. About what kind of relations we have. Finding us together that one time has made her damn curious."

"Not repelled?"

"Nay. Curious." Thomas took another second before he explained. "She caught me wincing, asked me about it, but I gave some vague excuse. Then I fell asleep, at least partly asleep. Evidently I mumbled that you'd ridden me too hard."

"And?" Rowan prompted, equally curious.

"She wouldn't stop questioning me about what I'd meant. Then when I blurted out that we'd fucked, she wanted to know *how* that could work." He watched Rowan's eyebrows shoot up in surprise. His lips twitched, which irritated Thomas. This wasn't a laughing matter. "She doesn't give up when she wants something. Stubborn woman."

Rowan nodded, still appearing amused. "She's going to make an interesting wife. A good one, I'm thinking." Thomas hoped they could work through their problems. He was still dealing with the way she constantly surprised him. "She got me so irritated with her concern about how things worked between us, in her worry about why I seemed to be in pain. I rolled over and pointed at my ass. God's teeth, can you believe I did that?"

"It's a great ass." Rowan grinned at him, trying to lighten the mood. "I admire it all the time."

For a second Thomas got distracted. His mind's eye saw Rowan's taut ass, pictured his lover waiting on all fours for him, and imagined his hands gripping Rowan's muscled body as he drove his cock deep into his tight butt hole. He shuddered with the desire that was beginning to weave through him. Then he forced it down. This was not the time to be thinking about fucking his friend.

Drawing in a steadying breath, he said, "The woman is a constant surprise to me." He thought back to their first day here, to their first conversation. "Remember how she meekly said she had no value as a woman or as a wife? How she seemed to fear you and me, because we were warriors…because we were men.

The memory still bothered him. From Rowan's frown, he knew his lover felt the same way. "Stewart abused her in many ways. May he rot in Hell for eternity."

"Yet she found the spirit to boldly tell you she would never allow a man to treat her like that again." Rowan smiled again, clearly admiring her daring. "She even went on to insist you look at more than her small stature. That you see her as able to perform the lord's wife's normal duties of running the keep, which evidently Stewart had not allowed."

Yes, Thomas remembered her annoyance at being considered unable to be taken seriously because of her almost child-like size. He couldn't help but worry about her, want to protect her from harm. Still, she had been acting as chatelaine for the year Stewart was gone from Middlemound. He would let her continue those duties, but he would be watching, ready to step in and assist her if needed. "She dreads my bedding her. Fears I will be cruel in some way, hurt her as Stewart did." Thomas curled his hands into fists at the thought of any man harming such a delicate little beauty in any manner. "She believes *she* failed that bastard; she failed in the role of wife."

"I've heard some talk about…" Rowan's jaw tightened and he cut off what he'd started to say. "Tis in her past and she needs your gentleness to heal those wounds that run soul-deep."

Thomas couldn't remember how many men he'd killed over his years of warring. He didn't want to think about it. His last battles in Tunis had nearly pushed him over the edge. But Rowan had saved him. *Thank God.* Still, he was troubled by the kind of man he was, by the life he'd led. "*My* gentleness?" he questioned in disbelief. "I'm a warrior. All I've known for years is battling, maiming, killing. What do I know of 'gentleness'?"

Rowan's eyes heated in desire and in defense. "Aye, you may be a man with strong passions for warring and leading your men. But you've a fierce passion for loving as well. This I know from experience. She needs to see your passionate side." He gave a crooked smile, the heat in his gaze flaming higher. "Mayhap toning down the intensity of your passion at first."

His lover looked thoughtful for a second. "I believe there is a loving woman hidden beneath the cautious exterior Gloriana shows to the world. I saw the way she melted into your kiss after the wedding ceremony. I saw the curiosity in her eyes, the hope." Thomas had sensed it, too, prayed he could find the strength to be gentle with her and give her time to accept that he wouldn't hurt her. He would have to save his need for rougher sex for his times with Rowan. His cock began to show interest for that, so he forced his thoughts back to last night and the other way in which his wife had surprised him.

Again he looked around to be sure no one had wandered within hearing range. Satisfied they were still alone, he said, "My timid wife surprised me yet again last night. After I pointed at my ass and all but said that's the way we fucked, she actually pushed my butt cheeks apart to look more closely."

He recalled his distress at the examination, his shock that she would do so. Yet, later as he'd drifted off to sleep, he'd also recalled how gentle her fingers had been on his bare ass. He'd hardened just thinking about it and had fought the desire to make love to his wife. The timing had been wrong.

Rowan watched him, waiting for him to finish what he'd started to say. He shoved aside his musings. "When she found my butt hole red and obviously sore, she was determined to apply one of her salves." He snorted. "I refused. I told her to leave my ass alone."

Rowan laughed so hard he had to hold his sides. When some of the men across the bailey glanced over, Thomas glowered at them until they looked away, and then he scowled at Rowan.

"Do you want *me* to tell her to leave your ass alone? Tell her that it is mine to worry about…mine to touch…mine to…" He faced Thomas, lowering his voice again. "Mine alone to fuck."

"This is *not* funny. It was embarrassing." Thomas narrowed his eyes. "How would you like it if she'd touched you in such a manner? Tried to—"

"I'd have let her do whatever she wanted with me," Rowan said seriously. He sighed, looked away. "She cares about you, even after what you told her about not wanting to get her with child. You're a damn lucky man." Thomas nodded. "I am and I don't deserve her."

Rowan didn't respond, instead he glanced across the bailey, and then moved in that direction. "Time I go back to training. Some of these Middlemound soldiers need much instruction."

Watching his friend walk away, Thomas considered his words 'do whatever she wanted with me' and 'you're a damn lucky man.' He'd never heard Rowan sound so interested in a woman before. He wasn't sure what to think about the matter. Gloriana was *his* wife. Rowan was his lover. They each held a special place within him. Could he share his wife with his lover? Could he share his lover with his wife? The whole idea was strange to him, not repulsive. Yet having sex with a man that first time had been strange, too. Again, he hadn't been repulsed by what they had done. He'd have to think more on this situation, see how things developed.

***

Gloriana's nose started to twitch, her eyes watering in preparation for a sneeze. Frantically she covered her nose. She absolutely could *not* sneeze now! Blessedly, the urge went away as fast as it had come upon her, and she remained in the shadows just inside the paddock. She'd come out here to check on her mare, who had injured her leg during a short ride the previous week. Then she'd become trapped here when Thomas and Rowan had walked up to have a private talk.

She peeked around the small wall that kept her hidden from the two men. Rowan was walking away, at last. Thomas stood there another minute, then finally he, too, walked off. She breathed a sigh of relief. *Oh my, what she'd heard! So much to take in and think about.* She'd heard the longing and the frustration in her husband's voice as he'd talked about his son. She needed to know more of their history. She couldn't bear the idea of father and son being kept apart any longer, for whatever the original reason. She would find a way to fix this situation for them both. James did *not* belong to Abernon! And if Thomas wouldn't give her a child of her own, at least she might be able to mother his son James.

Her heart pinched at that thought. She had enough love within her for this boy she had yet to meet, but she still ached to have a child borne of her body. Her eyes misted and she blinked away the tears. She would not give up hope, not give up her dream this easily.

Across the bailey Rowan accepted a wooden practice sword from another soldier. He immediately went into attack position, the muscles in his body hardening, capturing her attention. He moved with such grace, with such agility. A warrior clear to the bone, as was her new husband. Thomas, too, had a well-toned body that held her interest. In truth, she wanted to touch it, wanted to run her hands over his chest, see what his chest hair felt like. She'd never wanted to touch Geoffrey, though he'd forced her to do so.

Her face heated at what Thomas had told Rowan about last night. How could she have been so daring? Rolling him over so she could spread his butt cheeks, feeling sorry for the pain he suffered, wanting to put salve on his tender, puckered hole. Yet she would do all of it again. She didn't like the idea of anyone being in pain. Mayhap she should speak to Rowan. Tell him to take more care the next time he 'pounded' her husband. Why did the fact that Thomas and Rowan 'fucked'—as Thomas had told her—not bother her? Why did she so easily accept such a strange thing? In truth, the idea of it made her feel odd, tingly, achy. A naughty side she hadn't known she even had was intrigued, wished to observe this unique behavior, this intense passion Rowan had spoken of.

*Passion.* Rowan believed Thomas to be a very passionate man. She didn't actually fear him touching her or bedding her, and she didn't really fear that he would hurt her. She'd seen the way his eyes had warmed when he looked at her. She'd felt the tenderness, the heat in his kiss. She'd felt the solid ridge of his rod as it rubbed against her. She wouldn't disappoint him in their bedchamber again. She would not foolishly faint again.

Rowan spun around, waving his sword, muscles rippling. Warmth curled within her. *Desire. For Rowan?* Yes, she was definitely fascinated by the man in many ways. She'd seen the secrets hidden in his eyes, the hurt buried there. It called to her, a need to help him make peace with whatever troubled him. And she enjoyed looking at his fine warrior's body. But she was married to Thomas, and she would never dishonor him by encouraging Rowan in any manner. Besides, Rowan was Thomas's lover. She didn't want to intrude on that relationship. This was all so very confusing: her strange wariness and desire for both Thomas and Rowan, the intimacy the two men shared, her curiosity about it.

Moving out of the shadows, she felt a fluttering in her stomach. Thomas would bed her this day. And this day she *would not* embarrass herself by fainting before he could do it!

***

The great hall was packed with soldiers, servants and a number of the wives and children of his men. There was hardly an available space on the long benches by the trestle tables. Laughter echoed around the large room as the men taunted and teased one another after enduring a hard day of training. Mugs of ale thudded on the tables as they were set down. Higher pitched youthful voices competed for the attention of their parents. Weary mothers tried to deal with tired children. All of it was more than Thomas could stand another minute longer. He wanted to be alone with his bride, ached to take her to his bed.

He slid yet another glance in her direction. Gloriana looked especially pretty tonight. She wore a green gown that matched her eyes, a gown with a low bodice, low enough that her breasts were barely contained. He longed to free them, to cup them, to taste them. Once again he inhaled her scent, something soft, something flowery. She'd taken a bath earlier and must have used a special soap. He knew little about flowers, so he didn't know what it was, but whatever the floral smell was, it was driving him crazy.

Finally he could take no more of this torturous waiting. He hadn't eaten more than a couple of bites of the roasted swan the cook had prepared specially for them tonight. He'd not been able to even touch the fresh bread or the sweet date pie either, though they smelled good. He noted that Gloriana, too, had hardly nibbled at anything in her trencher.

He put his hand on hers where it rested on the table. So small, so soft. She jerked in surprise and looked warily at him. He saw the way her breasts rose and fell in quick little breaths. *Panic? Fear?* Both ideas sickened him. But then her gaze warmed and she blushed prettily.

Relief let him breathe easier. "I would ask that you go upstairs with me now, my lady." Those green eyes widened and he heard the catch in her breath, but she didn't pull away from him or refuse.

As they rose from their chairs at the table on the raised dais a number of the nearby soldiers glanced in their direction. Including Gerald, who narrowed his eyes. Thomas understood the protective man's silent warning to be careful with his lady. He would be irritated should any other man look at him in such a manner, but he truly didn't mind that this older man watched after her like a worried father. He'd heard the man had intervened as often as he could between Gloriana and Geoffrey, at the risk of keeping his position and probably even his life. He respected the knight greatly for that.

He shifted his glance to his right, where Rowan sat next to him. They hadn't spoken since their awkward morning conversation, and he worried a bit about his friend's odd quietness this night. Rowan still didn't speak and Thomas couldn't decipher the odd expression he wore. *Envy? Jealousy?* He wasn't sure. He didn't see the pinched lines on Rowan's forehead which showed when he was angry. For that, Thomas was grateful. Before he turned away, though, he said in concern, "I'll talk with you on the morrow."

Rowan gave a slight nod and focused on the food in front of him. "Aye. We need to discuss plans for dealing with Abernon."

*Abernon. His son.* Just the thought of some kind of upcoming battle made Thomas sick. He didn't want to cause problems for his sister, but he wanted his son…needed his son.

Gloriana surprised him yet again by gently touching his arm and making him face her. Her eyes mirrored determination, even a tinge of anger. "You will get your son, my lord. I truly believe that." Her fierce support touched places within him that had been long cold. Only Rowan had stood solidly by him for this last half year. Before that

Thomas had had many allies and many men willing to fight with him, but none he could call a real friend. He wasn't as religious as some of his men, yet he felt blessed by coming back physically whole from the Crusade, by having Rowan as a devoted first knight and lover, and now at having married a woman who intrigued him as much as she attracted him.

It was the attraction tightening within him that had him putting her hand in the crook of his arm and leading her out of the great hall. As she took the stairs in front of him, his body thrummed with desire. He prayed he could find the inner strength to be patient, to hold back an animalistic need to claim her. He curled his hands into fists when the urge to reach for her nearly overpowered him. Lust was not a new feeling for him, but this time was different. After years of bedding more women than he could even remember, he was taking a wife to his bed. He didn't think he could survive losing another wife. Nay, he could not give her the babe she longed to have. There were many ways to prevent his wife from becoming pregnant, for tonight he would put his faith in the special tea mixed with Queen Anne's lace he'd already had a maid prepare and take to their chamber.

They had reached the second floor with the bedchambers and solar when Gloriana stopped and timidly met his gaze. He watched her swallow hard, watched her raise her small chin and straighten her slender shoulders. He waited for her to speak, though he was anxious to go to their chamber.

"I will not faint on you this time, my lord. You need not fear that."

She drew in a shaky breath. "I will let you have your way with me without protest." *Let him have his way?* "This is not only about my wants and needs, Gloriana. It is about what we both desire, about pleasuring both of us."

He found it charming the way her cheeks grew pink at the idea of pleasuring one another. He couldn't wait another second to touch her in some way. He cupped her face and slowly lowered his mouth to hers. She held her breath, tensed, but met his lips tentatively at first. And then she shivered and inched closer to him. She gave a soft moan as he lightly trailed his tongue along the seam of her lips.

His cock had hardened painfully, and it pressed between them, pressed against her. She quietly sighed but didn't shift away. He shuddered and kissed her harder, demanding a response from her. To his delight, she put her delicate hands on the sides of his face and kissed him back.

When he could find the strength to pull away, he did. His breaths came hard and his heart pounded. He held her desire-heavy gaze and said huskily, "I promise to be gentle, my wife."

Her chin lifted again and she boldly countered, "I would like to experience some of this passion Rowan claims you have." With that said, she turned to march into their bedchamber.

Thomas stood there stunned. *Passion? Rowan told her he had 'passion'?* When? When would his friend have told her such a thing? Something nagged at him, but…

She stepped back into the doorway, interrupting his musing. An irritated look pinched her face. "Husband? What keeps you there?"

He shook off his shock and grinned. "Nothing."

"You really need to work on that smile, Thomas. Tis rather odd; not exactly scary, but odd." Then she scurried farther into the chamber.

Thomas was still grinning when he closed and locked the door behind him. She had already moved next to the bed and lit one of the candles on a bedside table. The mug of tea sat beside the candle. *Good.* Relief filled him.

"I have had little to smile about in a very long time. I will work on it."

Although she had come up here with no resistance, even been brazen but a moment ago, the color had left her face. She'd begun trembling. He went to her and pulled her into a hug they both needed. She fit him perfectly. He liked that her head rested just below his chin, liked the way her plump breasts pressed against him. He especially liked the way her arms moved around him and held him in trust and not fear.

"I need help getting out of this gown," she said nervously. "I can call a maid."

"Nay, my lady, I will gladly act your maid this night." He released her and turned her around so he could untie the lacing on the back of her gown. It was difficult work with his big fingers, but he'd undressed many other women over the years. This was his wife, though. It was very different this time.

He'd begun to lose patience with the tedious task when finally the gown started to slide off her shoulders. Creamy skin took his breath away. She didn't wear an undergarment, which surprised him, which made him all the more ready to get the gown completely off her. He pulled it down slowly, almost drooling as he revealed more and more of her soft, perfect skin. She stood still, letting him undress her, trusting him.

God in heaven, how could she trust him after what she'd been through with Geoffrey? It humbled him.

When she stood naked in front of him with her gown pooled at her feet, he simply stared at her. She was beautiful. Tinier than other women he'd been with. He felt overly big and prayed he wouldn't crush her when he stretched over her.

She faced him, her cheeks pink in embarrassment. She had trouble meeting his eyes. "Do I disgust you, my lord? Am I too…"

"Disgust me? Good God, no!"

She stepped out of the gown at her small feet, toed off the slippers and pushed them away. "Geoffrey found me too small for his taste. He could hardly stand to be with me." Her voice was a miserable whisper.

"The man was not only a cruel bastard, but a fool." Thomas looked down at her and felt nervous. He'd never felt anxious with other women. Again, she was his wife. "Mayhap it is I who will displease you. I am too big, too—"

She reached up to put a finger to his mouth, stopping his worried admission. "Nay, my lord, you do not displease me. At least not because you are far bigger than me. My concern lies more with whether or not your…" She looked down and her face reddened. "With whether your rod will fit inside me. I have seen it and twas rather large. Impressively large."

His shaft swelled at the compliment, swelled and ached. He tugged his tunic off. "My rod will fit just fine. I have great faith in that."

Her eyes had darkened as she stared at his chest. "You've many scars, too many. You've suffered great pain."

"None more than I suffer at this moment."

He shoved off his braies and freed his cock, which he was sure had never been as hard or as long as it was now. She gaped at the size of it, but couldn't take her gaze away. That pleased him even more. He took his length in one hand, stroked it once, and caught the heat in her eyes. "I cannot wait much longer to slide inside you, wife." "Can…can I touch it?" She reached for him, but hesitated.

"Aye," he choked out the word. He hoped he wouldn't disgrace himself at the touch of her hand. When she still hesitated, he took her hand and wrapped it around him. Cautiously at first, she moved her hand up and down his shaft. She watched in clear amazement as it grew even bigger within her hold. She grew bolder, stroking with more fervor, smiling up at him. "Your rod, it doesn't shrink at my touch. It grows. Tis magic, my lord."

"Just the magic of your touch, wife," he groaned, struggling to keep his thoughts sane, to not toss her onto the bed and drive deep. Her comment found its way into his mind, puzzled him. Stewart's cock had withered at her touch? What had been wrong with the man? His rod felt as if it would explode from how big it had grown. Fearing that he would release prematurely, he gently pulled her hand away.

"Before you unman me, I would have you lie on the bed. Let me prepare you, bring you pleasure before I drive into your sweet body."

The disappointment he first saw in her face as he removed her hand from his cock transformed into anticipation. "Prepare me? Bring me pleasure?" she questioned in wonder. In that moment, he knew her first husband had taken no time to prepare her before he rammed into her depths. He'd never brought her pleasure. *The bastard.*

"Trust me, Gloriana." He didn't want to explain; he wanted to show her what he'd meant.

"I do." Her whispered response touched him deeply.

As she started to move toward the bed, his gaze darted to the mug of tea. Guilt fluttered within him, yet he almost desperately went to pick up the mug and handed it to her. He could not meet her eyes as he said, "I had the maid prepare you a special tea, something to quench your thirst before I have my way with you."

Her eyebrows pinched in curiosity, but she drained the mug. "Twas different, my lord, but good. I thank you for your consideration."

She sat on the bed and he finally realized her hair was still wrapped in complicated braids about her head. His focus had been only on the exquisite body that so tempted him. Gruffly he said, "I would have you take your hair down. I wish to see it flowing around you."

Within seconds she'd released the waist-length mass of blonde hair and sat looking at him. "In all fairness, husband, I would ask that you remove the leather tying your hair back as well."

He did so and was pleased to see her eyes warm as she watched his hair fall around his shoulders. No other woman had ever seemed to care if his hair was tied back or loose. "Happy now, Glori?"

She blinked at him at the shortened name and then nodded with a slight smile. Then without being instructed to do so, she scooted backward on the bed, with the fur cover and linen already pulled down to the end. She stopped to pull her long hair to one side before lying back and putting her head on the pillows. Her plump breasts rose and fell with her anxious breaths as she waited for him.

"You wish me to spread my legs wide? Or to raise them at the knees? Tell me what you desire, my lord, and I will obey." Tentatively, she shifted her slender legs apart. His body forgot all about breathing. She was such an innocent in so many ways. She'd been brutalized in her marital bed; he knew this without her admitting as much. Yet she now trusted him, a stranger. It made him dig deep for patience. He could not hurt her.

# Chapter Five

Gloriana watched her new husband as he stood there tall, so big, and so sinfully handsome. She wondered why she didn't feel the fear she'd always experienced before Geoffrey had mounted her. Their mating had never been pleasant. He'd never talked about preparing her body, whatever that was. He'd never cared about anything but finding his own satisfaction. And he'd rarely found it, for which she'd paid dearly. She trembled at the memory of the last beating he'd given her for failing him. The physical wounds had healed; the emotional ones would probably always be with her. It was difficult to trust another man and yet she did.

"Do not think of Stewart. Never again," Thomas said gruffly, anger and gentleness an odd mix in his tone. "I will never hurt you. Never."

She drew in a breath and studied him for a second. His jaw had tightened and a vein pulsed in his neck. This man was so much harder, so much more powerful than Geoffrey had been. But instinctively she knew *this* man never misused his strength, never abused the power he held over anyone. Unless they were an enemy, of course. An enemy would see a side of him she hoped never to witness. Yet still she did not fear him. Even in this short a time she had seen the respect for him in his men's expressions, even seen the beginnings of it in Middlemound's men.

Deciding to have faith in the man looking down at her with such grim determination, she held out her arms. "Come make me your wife, my lord. Geoffrey will not come between us any longer." It was a promise she hoped to keep.

Relief settled over Thomas's face and he gave a curt nod. The feather mattress dipped as he knelt on it and crawled toward her, moving slowly between her legs. His eyes darkened, heated, held such clear desire. It was truly wondrous to see such longing for her. Her own body came alive. Her woman's place quivered and the small bud between her legs throbbed. Her breasts felt fuller, ached. *Want.* She *wanted* this man. Never had she felt this way. Well, maybe a little of such feelings when she gazed upon Rowan. But her desire for Thomas was far stronger.

"I must touch your breasts." His voice had lowered an octave. His gaze melded to her chest. "I must taste those hard nubs calling to me."

*Yes, she wanted that, too.* Her pulse raced. She inhaled the scent of him, one of musk with a faint hint of sweat. The day was hot and he'd been busy most of it. She didn't mind at all. In a second of daring, she cupped her breasts as if offering them to him.

He drew in a breath and his eyes widened in delight. He moved until he knelt above her. So big, so brawny. His shoulders seemed twice as wide as hers. The mass of his body was so much bigger than hers. But his size didn't intimidate her. She froze, not in fear but in wonder. His long, solid rod lay on her stomach, rubbed just over her mound and sent tingles clear down to her toes. His intense focus remained on her breasts, which she still held, they seemed to have swollen even more.

With a growl low in his throat, he reached toward her and took each plump breast from her hands into his. She watched him, held her breath, tensed for the kind of pain she'd always experienced before. She waited for him to harshly squeeze the mounds, waited for him to bend down and bite the nipples, and waited for him to gloat at the control he had over her.

Instead Thomas gently held her breasts as if they were rare treasures. He met her uncertain gaze. His look told her she'd given him a special gift.

"They're very nice, my wife. Precious." He lowered his head and swirled his tongue around one nipple, before grinning up at her. She'd gone stiff, surprised by the incredible sensation of his raspy tongue circling her sensitized skin. There was no pain, only pleasure. "You may do that again," she said on a purr. She desperately *needed* him to do it again.

"I may?" he questioned, his lips tipping up in amusement. His hands tenderly massaged her breasts.

Her face had heated at her boldness, but his amusement made her bolder. "Aye, you may do that again and again. Although I believe you should not neglect one breast for the other." Now his eyes mirrored his enjoyment at her daring. He flicked his thumbs over the nubs, which immediately hardened. "You are right. I should show no partiality to one delightful breast over another."

This man who seldom smiled, who rarely even appeared happy, was teasing her. She liked it. He was far too serious. Such a softening in behavior was good for him. "So what do you plan to do about the matter?"

"Give adequate attention to each sweet breast, of course."

He lowered his head and she grew tense again in anticipation. His warm, wet mouth drew a nipple into it. He didn't bite down cruelly as Geoffrey had done. No, that wondrous tongue circled it again and again, danced across the very tip, and then his teeth lightly held it for but a second. Still there was no pain, only pleasure.

She arched upward, sighing with exquisite enjoyment. "Tis magic, this thing you do."

He chuckled and moved to give equal attention to her other breast. This time he drew the nipple more firmly between his lips, suckling as she'd seen babes do at their mother's breasts. It was such a strange feeling, a very enjoyable one.

Gloriana clasped his head, wove her fingers through his long dark hair, and held him to her. "Tis so very nice, this suckling." She arched her back and wanted more. "Do not neglect the other nipple, my lord," she said on a sigh. She heard what sounded like a grunt of approval, and he slid his tongue around the nipple a final time before lifting his head, causing her to release him. Glancing at her for but an instant, he shifted to the other breast. She held him to her with more force this time, not wishing the amazing sensations to end. Tears misted her eyes even as anger curled inside her. Geoffrey had robbed her of these pleasures. Just when she wasn't sure she could take any more of these unfamiliar yet beautiful sensations, Thomas moved back. His eyes held such a satisfied look.

"Thank you, my lady, for allowing me such an honor."

Her breasts were still swollen, the nipples still hard. "I could 'honor' you more, my lord." *That wasn't exactly begging, was it?* Although she *was* tempted to beg for the experience again.

He shook his head and his hair brushed his shoulders, making her want to reach out and feather her fingers through it. He didn't say a word, but his eyes darkened even more and he shifted and placed a hand over her hairy mound. His fingers dangled between her legs. She sucked in a shuddery breath as those fingers lightly tapped where they lay, her lower lips seemed to pulse more and more. Wetness trickled from between those lips, something she'd never before experienced. *Is it wrong? Would he not like it?* She could do nothing about the reaction, but wait and worry.

"Tis all right, Glori. Relax," his voice was husky. He moved his hand again, reached between her legs and found those beads of moisture that concerned her. He stroked his fingers there, coated them with the wetness.

She barely breathed, anxious for his reaction.

Then he looked up at her, his expression pleased as he continued to play with her lips. He did not disapprove. Relief washed over her and she allowed herself to enjoy what he was doing. "You do not mind that my body…"

"Tis a natural reaction." He furrowed his brow. "Have you not experienced it before?"

Gloriana couldn't meet his eyes, could only shake her head. Nay, she had not.

He grumbled a curse, angry once again with Geoffrey. Yet his anger was only in what he said, not in what he did. Ever so gently he slid a long finger inside her, and then added a second one. "My lord, what are you doing?" she asked on a gasp. His fingers moved inside her. His thumb found her pulsing bud and played with it. She couldn't keep from rocking upward. Muscles inside her woman's place squeezed around his invading fingers and claimed them. She didn't want them to ever stop what they were doing. "I wished to make sure you were ready for me. *This* is the preparation I spoke of before." His look of male pride grew. "Your body responds well to me. I do not think either of us can wait any longer. Another time I will give you even more pleasure."

Gloriana was nearly lost in a haze of feeling. "Even more pleasure? How can there be more?" She sighed and concentrated on those wonderful, magical fingers moving inside her. "I like this thing you call 'preparation.'"

"There can be much more pleasure, my sweet innocent," he said on a shaky groan and then pulled his fingers from her body. He sat back on his bent legs.

Annoyance made her scowl at him. "What are you doing? I need—"

"*This* is what you truly need, wife." He took hold of his long, firm rod, and she could only stare at it. Then he stroked his hand up and down the length, his expression appearing strained.

She remembered how hard his shaft had felt in her hand, how silky soft as well. Still, she worried about such a large cock being forced into her body. She nibbled anxiously at her lower lip.

"Do not be afraid." He bent over and carefully put the head to her slit, and then inched it barely inside her. "Twill be all right." He braced his powerful arms at her sides and slowly eased farther into her body.

She remembered only horrible pain when Geoffrey entered her body. He'd taken no care with her. He'd held her firmly in place and bruised her thighs with his roughness. Then he'd rammed as deep as he could go in one long painful thrust. Yet she felt none of that this time, not even a twinge of pain.

Surprised and curious, she leaned up until she could see Thomas's thick shaft disappearing into her body a bit at a time. He was so gentle, yet persistent. Although she'd feared it would never fit, her body was adjusting with only minimal discomfort. *Truly amazing.* She found herself smiling at him. "You were right. It does fit."

His handsome face appeared taut with strain now from the obvious effort of moving slowly. She didn't like that she was causing him pain of any kind. She would not allow it. Determined to stop his suffering, she wrapped her legs around him and pulled him down, forcing his rod deeper. She gave a small gasp.

"I would have *all* of you. Now," she demanded, giving him a determined smile when he glanced in concern at her. "I am not as delicate as you seem to think. I can take your great length. I *want* it!"

"Then you shall have me." He filled her to the hilt, his pelvis grinding against hers. He grew still and searched her face, his eyes worried. "Are you all right?" *Was she?* She'd never felt such fullness, but she definitely liked it. "Is this where you show your passion, my lord? When your rod drives into who you are loving at the moment?"

He had started moving, but stopped and studied her. "I cannot believe Rowan talked to you about passion, about *my* passion. That troubles me. I will have a stern talk with him."

Gloriana worried her lip for a second, squeezed her inner muscles around his girth, and admitted quietly, "He did not talk to me about it." At Thomas's raised eyebrows, she felt her face heat and she looked away. "I was in the paddock earlier, before you and Rowan went there. I didn't mean to intrude on your privacy, truly I didn't. But I was already there. I...I heard you two talking." Irritation flashed over his face and she tensed. Would he be angry enough now to beat her? She waited anxiously.

His shoulders sagged, and he blew out a breath. "I do not like eavesdropping, Gloriana, know that. But, in this instance, I understand. You are forgiven."

As if he couldn't remain still another second, he began pumping his hips in slow, deep strokes. She trembled as each one sent shivers throughout her. She started to writhe beneath him.

"He loves you, Rowan does." She felt compelled to remind Thomas of that. "He doesn't want me to hurt you, believes I can help you."

Thomas shuddered above her, his face tense with strain as he continued to thrust inside her. He pulled nearly out and then thrust deep again, over and over. Yet he studied her and finally said, "I love him, too. I pray that won't be a problem between us. But I cannot give him up."

He pulled nearly out again, held there a second. "I wish to have you both in my life, take you both to my bed." With that said, he drove deep once more.

She could barely think straight from the feelings assailing her. She'd never thought to experience such pleasure, never wanted to do without it again. She had great desire for this powerfully built husband of hers. If Rowan felt anything close to the wonders she now experienced, he would not want to give Thomas up either. And she respected Thomas for admitting the depth of his feelings for his friend. He was indeed a loyal and passionate man. A truly wonderful lover.

She remained silent, losing herself to his lovemaking, climbing higher and higher with him. Her thoughts were scattering. She began moaning, began moving in tandem with him. "Oh…oh, Thomas. I…I…"

He pounded relentlessly into her, and she eagerly welcomed it. She bucked beneath him and pulled him ever closer with her legs wrapped around him. How much longer could she take this? She couldn't breathe a full breath. She needed… *What?* She had no idea what she needed.

On yet another fierce drive inside her, she cried out, "Thomas! Oh, husband!" Then the most surprising thing happened to her. She stiffened, held her breath. More moisture exploded from her body, more even than when Thomas had teased and tortured her with his fingers. "Ohhh, oh Thomas!"

Her heart pounded. She felt so amazingly content. It was hard to take in, having never felt anything like this before. It almost frightened her, the power of this feeling. As she lay there panting, her leg muscles quivered, and she dropped her legs from around him.

But Thomas didn't stop moving. His face contorted with pain while he pounded into her several more times, frantically, deeper and deeper. At last he threw his head back and growled her name as his hot cream shot inside her. She felt so full with it. Again, this was a new experience. Geoffrey hadn't… *No! You must stop comparing Thomas to Geoffrey!*

Gloriana forced her dead husband from her thoughts. Only Thomas mattered now. She tenderly cupped his face, thumbed away the beads of sweat on his cheeks. Even though he did not want to get her with child, she hoped he'd done so. She very much would like to bear this big, complicated man a babe. With that notion in her mind, she hardly noticed him leaving her body, moving to stretch out beside her.

She closed her eyes in utter happiness, dreaming of a little girl with her blonde hair and with Thomas's deep blue eyes.

***

Rowan tossed and turned during the long night. He knew what his lover had done, knew that at last Thomas had bedded his new bride. He could almost smell the aftereffects of their lovemaking clear at his end of the hallway. He did not resent their finally coming together, nor did he feel jealous. No, it was more a feeling of being left out.

Finally he tossed the linen covering aside and climbed from his bed to pace naked around his darkened bedchamber. Thomas had been his lover for six months, and he was afraid to lose him now that his friend's life had taken this turn. Rowan knew he could find another man to sake his lust with, but no other man appealed to him anymore. He enjoyed just looking at Thomas's body, all iron-muscled and sinewy. He liked caressing those hard chest muscles, feeling Thomas's corded arms moving around him in a hug. He liked seeing Thomas bend over and offer his taut butt to him to fuck. And he desperately enjoyed bending over for Thomas to drive his large, thick cock into his ass. No, there was no other man who could ever satisfy him the way Thomas did.

He'd had sex with many women over the years, but he wasn't driven by a fierce need to bed a woman like some men were. Even Thomas was sometimes driven to take a woman to his bed. It had happened in some of the small towns they'd been in during their travels. Thomas was passionate, his needs for sex strong. Rowan hadn't minded when Thomas went off with a woman, because his lover had always still come back to him. Rowan had never wanted to have the intense kind of sex with a woman that Thomas shared with him. That Thomas now shared with Gloriana.

*Gloriana.* She was such a small woman to be married to such a large man. And she'd been abused, verbally as much as physically, or so he'd gathered from pieces of talk he'd overheard. The people of Middlemound were watching Thomas, hoping he would be a far better husband to their lady than Stewart had been. So far they seemed to accept him, especially after his concern for her when she'd fainted. All knew he hadn't forced an immediate marriage, and he hadn't forced bedding her after her fainting spell.

Stopping to look out the arrow-slit window toward the moonlit night, he wrapped his hand around his aching shaft. Thomas would not be coming to him this night. He'd heard his lover's bellow when he'd found relief within Gloriana. Rowan didn't mind that; was, in fact, pleased it had happened. Yet it did nothing to slake the lust he felt, the need tearing at him. If he wanted to, he could seek out Marie. She wouldn't turn him away, but he didn't want that tonight. Instead he worked his rod here in the near-darkness. He pulled steadily on it, missing the way Thomas did it, missing having Thomas's warm mouth move over it. His friend was a masterful lover, and a good man at heart. He was fiercely loyal to the men who pledged under him. There were few warriors better than he. And, once he managed to settle into the role, Thomas would make a good lord here and a great husband for Gloriana. He would never hurt her, at least not physically. His hand moved faster. His breaths came harder. Heat spiraled through him, aching desperation, too. He pulled and smoothed his fingers again and again tight around the pulsing shaft. *Soon. It had to come soon.*

He rocked his body into the frantic movements. *Gloriana.* Even though he shouldn't be thinking of her, she popped into his fevered thoughts. She was the first woman he could ever recall that drew him. He ached to lay a claim to her body. But he couldn't.

Pumping harder still, he gritted his teeth in the agony of almost reaching the point of release. He had much experience with using his hand, but he would have preferred being buried deep within a warm body. His pulse raced and he began shuddering.

He thought of heat surrounding his cock, tightness pulling at it. He could only imagine the pleasure of being held inside Gloriana's moist depths. And he knew the intense pleasure he would have found inside Thomas's ass. *Oh God! So close now.* He jerked on his rod, frantically. His mind's eye saw Gloriana before him on all fours, with that mass of soft, blonde hair draped around her. He would cover her from behind like a stallion covering his mare. She would whimper a bit, hold herself still and wait for him to drive his cock into her. Her sweet body would tremble, but she would push back against him in her desperate demand for more.

He stiffened, sweating, holding his rod for a second as it throbbed within his hand hold. His eyes closed and he saw himself giving her begging body what she wanted. He rode her until they both went crazy. She screamed out his name and he roared out hers.

His hand squeezed and pulled a final time. Warm cum flowed over his hand. Twas a shame he could not pour his life force into Gloriana's body. He would have no problem getting her with child. He did not have the same fears Thomas did. He would enjoy seeing her swell with a babe in her belly.

Once he had the strength to move again, he reached for a rag on the nearby chest and wiped the stickiness from his body. He would never see her growing with babe. She would never have the experience she longed for because Thomas couldn't bring himself to endanger her life that way. And he would never touch her. That didn't stop him from fantasizing about her, though. Or fantasizing about the three of them together.

***

A week had passed since Thomas had sent his men to Abernon. The waiting for news was wearing on him; wearing on his people in Middlemound as well. He couldn't tell them what was bothering him. He couldn't tell them that, if necessary, he would be taking men to his sister's home and possibly battling there. It shamed him to know he had a son and had abandoned him for nearly all of his life. Yes, he'd left James with his sister because he'd known she would love the boy as if he were one of her own children, yet he felt weak because he hadn't been able to face raising a child on his own, or up to finding another wife to raise his son while he went off to war as he had long done. But ashamed of his past behavior or not, he wanted his son. He needed a chance to make things right between them.

He looked toward the gardens where Gloriana pulled vegetables for the day's sup. He had another wife now. Every day he learned more about this tiny woman he'd married. Like she'd told him, she might be small in stature, but she was not a weak woman. She worked as hard about the keep as any of the staff, though he still watched in secret to make sure she didn't overdo. She did well in the role of chatelaine. Stewart had been a fool in so very many ways. His hands still longed to curl around the man's neck and twist the life from it for what he'd done to Gloriana.

One of the cook's grandchildren skipped by close to the garden and called out to his wife. She glanced up and gave the little girl one of her gentle smiles. The castle's many children all loved her. She teased and chased the little ones around the bailey from time to time. She laughed so easily. She'd even made him laugh a time or two.

His chest filled with pride just watching her. All here at Middlemound adored her, as did he. She'd blossomed now that she was free of Stewart and made love to daily by him. Rowan had been right; his wife was a very passionate woman. She'd just never been allowed to experience it until now.

He heard footsteps in the hard dirt coming up from behind him and drew in the familiar scent. *Rowan.*

Rowan stopped next to him and followed the direction of his gaze. "You've been good for her, my friend. Tis rare to see pain in Gloriana's eyes these days. She smiles freely now, shares her warmth with all around her." "Aye, she does." Thomas admired the way her sweet bottom wiggled as she bent over to tug a stubborn carrot from the earth. He shifted to adjust his instant erection. He'd gotten used to having to do so since their first bedding. He felt guilty for only having sought Rowan out four times this past week. But his wife took to loving well. She'd proved to be demanding in bed, which he certainly didn't mind. Still, he missed the powerful ways in which he and Rowan came together. He was afraid of being as forceful with her.

He faced his first knight, and his breath caught at seeing Rowan's bare, heavily muscled chest. His fingers ached to touch him, to wipe at the sweat beading his nearly hairless chest. The day was hot and Rowan, as some of the other men, had chosen to practice without the hot chainmail and undershirts. "I want you," he said huskily, quietly, so no one could hear.

Rowan's eyes darkened, his nostrils flared as he, too, appeared to deal with a desperate longing. If they'd been alone, Thomas knew Rowan would have pulled him forward. He would have felt Rowan's lips pressed to his. They would have held one another for long minutes as the fire built between them. Then…

Thomas blew out a deep breath of frustration. They were not alone. Both had duties to attend to and long hours ahead before they could even consider coming together.

He forced his thoughts in another direction. "She continues to press me about having a baby. She refuses to accept my reasoning for not giving her one," he stated the problem he'd been dealing with. "And she is growing suspicious of the teas I insist she drink every night." He'd practically had to pour it down her throat last night.

"Teas?" Rowan cocked an eyebrow, his tone suspicious. "A tea to keep from allowing a babe to grow in her belly." Thomas would have to change methods to keep her from becoming pregnant. He hated the thought of withdrawing from her body before shooting his load into her. And he wasn't fond of wearing a sheath of snakeskin or sheepskin. "I could insist she dip a piece of wool in a mixture of ground dates, tree bark and honey and insert it into her body. She would not like it." Admittedly, he was disgusted at that idea as well. The tea was much simpler.

Rowan looked at him like he was a foolish man. "I suspect Gloriana would not do it. I can't see her using a douche of blood, herbs, oils and animal dung, either. Nor should you ask it of her." He ground his teeth in irritation. "Thomas, you…"

"Nay!" Thomas snapped and drew the attention of a pair of men walking toward the keep. Gloriana, too, stood and glanced in their direction. He sighed and lowered his voice, "I will not discuss the matter further. My decision has been made."

Frowning and shaking his head in disgust, Rowan turned and walked away without another word.

***

An hour later Gloriana stopped stirring the large pot of spicy venison stew in the kitchen. It was sweltering hot. Perspiration beaded her face, trickled down her back. She needed a breath of fresh air. More than that, though, she needed to find her husband. It had been bothering her how he'd snapped at Rowan in the bailey and then how his friend had turned and strode away in anger. It worried her that they argued. They'd seemed to grow distant this past week, and she worried about that, too. She wanted to know what was bothering them. She wanted to fix whatever it was, and she prayed she wasn't somehow the problem.

They needed each other. Thomas needed her as well. She could sense that in him, but he needed Rowan in a different way. "I will be back later," she told the cook, motioning one of the young maids over to take her place. "I must talk a bit with my husband."

The older woman gave her a saucy smile. "He's a fine-looking man, our new lord. Gruff at times, but never with you."

"He hasn't had an easy time of things. All he's known is warring." Gloriana tipped her chin up in his defense.

"Don't get all ruffled, my lady. I was not talking against your new husband. Many men are gruff." The cook gave her a sympathetic look. "Lord Thomas is a good man. All here know it. All here have seen the way he looks at you, the gentleness that comes over him."

She chuckled. "We've not missed how you brighten up when he enters a room. Tis clear there's strong feelings between you, even in such a short time." She winked. "Take as long as you need with him, my lady."

Gloriana caught the amused and envious glances of the three young maids nearby. Her face heated knowing they believed she was seeking Thomas out for more than a mere 'talk.' The notion wasn't half bad, and she wouldn't turn him down if he wanted to take her up to their bedchamber.

"I really do want to talk with him," she stated stubbornly and strode from the room to the accompaniment of more chuckles.

The search for her husband was frustrating. She checked the great hall, which was nearly empty at this time of afternoon. She checked their bedchamber, the solar, and even Rowan's chamber. Finally she went out onto the keep's steps and the hot sun bore down on her.

She stood on the top step and squinted to look around the area. A couple dozen of the men continued to practice with their wooden swords in the bailey. Another bunch of men worked with their horses in one way or another near the paddocks. Villagers came and went all around the shops lining the inner walls and crossed over the lowered drawbridge heading back to the village. But nowhere did she see signs of Thomas or of Rowan. Mayhap they were off somewhere together fixing whatever problem had come between them. Or mayhap they were off somewhere fucking, as Thomas had said they did. She was all right with that, as long as Rowan wasn't so hard on her husband this time. At some point she really did want to know about their lovemaking, mayhap even talk them into letting her watch them. She'd become very curious about the matter, even dreamt one night of observing them.

Tingles began low in her body at the naughty idea. What would her husband say if he knew where her thoughts wandered? How would he respond if she did truly ask about watching him and Rowan together?

"He rode out a short while ago, my lady," Rowan said, walking up from around the corner of the keep.

Gloriana jerked in surprise, putting a hand to her breast. "You caught me off guard, Sir Rowan."

"Sorry. One of the men who'd seen you searching the keep for Thomas told me a minute ago. I just thought I'd tell you he left. Sir Gerald rode with him. A couple of the serfs were having a problem and it required his mediation."

She found it odd that Rowan hadn't gone along as well. "Why did you not go with him instead of Sir Gerald, or with them?" She studied his face, noted the strained lines around his mouth. He wasn't happy, had seemed to grow unhappier each day of late. "What troubles you? Can I help in some way?"

Some of the tension lifted in his expression. His eyes lost some of their sadness and for the first time she noticed his bare chest. *God's teeth, he's a handsome man!* She found it no wonder Thomas was drawn to him. She couldn't help admiring him, feeling drawn to him as well. But wanting to touch him, even feel his lips on hers, was one matter, acting upon it an entirely other matter. She would not betray her husband that way, and she would not lead Rowan along a false path, either.

She didn't think he was going to answer, but finally he said, "We are having a difference of opinion at the moment, tis all. We will get past it." He looked away. "I hope."

Gloriana followed his gaze and spotted Marie carrying a basket of vegetables from the garden toward the kitchen. The woman smiled at him, and it was clear she would have liked him to come speak with her. But he merely nodded and didn't move.

"Marie likes you," Gloriana said, feeling strangely a bit jealous. Foolish, that. She was married to Thomas, liked her husband, and might even be starting to love him.

"She's a kind-hearted woman, like you." Rowan looked her way again. His eyes were heated now, as Thomas's got when he wanted her. "But she's *not* you." Frustration etched his face.

Her gaze widened at his bold statement and she didn't know what to say. "I…I…" "Do not worry, Gloriana, I will not act on my desire. I wouldn't hurt you. I couldn't hurt Thomas." The sadness had returned to his eyes, and he turned to walk slowly toward the men by the paddocks. Stunned, she gaped after him. *Good heavens!* Surely he didn't… But he bedded Marie, the maid had told her as much. No, he couldn't… He was Thomas's lover. Marie's lover. But he'd said…

She hurried back into the safety of the keep, stopping to let her eyes adjust to the dimness. Then she all but raced up the stairs to the privacy of her bedchamber. She felt a sudden need to hide away.

For the first time in over a week, Gloriana quietly turned away Thomas's attempt to make love that night. She claimed a headache. He'd been concerned, but he hadn't pressed her. In truth, guilt for feeling attracted in any manner to Rowan weighed heavily on her.

She snuggled against Thomas, aching for him; yet unwilling to take his tender loving when her thoughts kept straying to Rowan. She was fairly certain that she loved Thomas. But she had a strong fondness for Rowan as well. Both men had been seriously hurt by things in their pasts, of this she was certain, though neither had admitted as much. Both difficult men needed a woman's gentle healing. *She* wanted to heal them both. And she wanted to touch them both.

A tear trickled from the corner of one eye. Her life always seemed to be filled with problems difficult to overcome. She could *not* love two men.

## Chapter Six

Gloriana had slept restlessly for the last six nights, torn by desire for her husband and by a longing she shouldn't have for Rowan. Because of her torment she had been glad that her woman's time of the month had come, although it had been nothing like prior times. She'd almost decided to talk to the elderly cook about it, but decided the difference this time must be due to stress. Still, she'd been disappointed by even the limited spotting she'd experienced. It meant Thomas hadn't given her a babe like she desperately wanted. He'd started to keep his distance from her, partly, she knew, because she'd become so moody. He had even slept in another chamber—possibly Rowan's, she didn't know—the last couple of nights. She'd told him yesterday that her monthly had ended, but he hadn't joined her in their bed that night, either. Mayhap she'd been wrong; mayhap he didn't have as strong a feeling for her as she'd thought.

She rolled onto her stomach and clutched the pillow as the first rays of dawn began slipping in through the nearby window. Tears filled her eyes. She was too depressed to even think about getting out of bed to begin another day.

A movement next to her on the bed startled her. *Thomas? When had he come to their bed? How could she have not noticed?* But his scent drifted over her and her mood lightened. It was enough to know that he had finally returned to their bed.

She started to turn over to face him, but he stopped her with a hand to the middle of her back.

"Nay, stay as you are, wife." His tone was the deep, husky timbre that she'd missed hearing. He removed his hand and shifted so that he could pull the thin linen covering to the end of the bed.

"I will remove my chemise." Again, she attempted to turn over, intending to sit up. Again, he held her pressed to the mattress. He touched her long braid for a second, and then moved it to one side. While she shivered from that gentle touch, he shoved her long gown up and over her back, baring her buttocks. The cool air of early morning swept over her, and she felt wickedly exposed.

He caressed her bottom and the cheeks quivered in response. Tingles of longing shot through her. She savored his touch, every gentle caress. She'd missed him, missed their lovemaking. Her mound rubbed against the bed linen and the ache she felt grew more intense. She needed more. She needed him inside her, now.

She couldn't resist pushing her bottom back at him, although this was not a position they'd used before. She wasn't sure what to do. "Thomas," she sighed and pushed again at his hand still on her bottom.

He continued to smooth his hands over her tingling flesh and straddled her legs. "We've not made love this way, Glori," he said, sounding strained.

"I know, husband." She was curious, yet she was uncertain, too.

He trailed a long finger down the cleft of her buttocks, slipping it to her swollen lower lips. "I very much want to do this. Are you all right with it?"

"Aye," she gasped, squirming as his finger found her pulsing bud. "Aye! Do whatever you wish, my lord. But do it soon!"

Thankfully, he didn't make her beg again. His engorged rod moved against her from behind. She felt just the tip of it at her entrance and her stomach fluttered with nerves. Cautiously, she pushed back.

Without another word, he put an arm beneath her stomach to lift her just enough that he could drive into her in one smooth motion. She sucked in a breath, froze in place. *So full. So different from other times.* She trembled and adjusted quickly as he waited patiently behind her.

The desperate need to move spread through her. She wiggled her bottom against him. "My lord, you must do something! Move! Now!"

"As you wish, my lady," his words came out huskily.

Obeying her command, he shifted his other arm beneath her. The feel of him all around her only served to make her tremble in anticipation. Then one of his magical fingers found her clit at the same time he began to steadily thrust in and out of her.

Gloriana's thoughts scattered, lost in the whirlwind of sensations spinning through her. His long, thick rod drove deep over and over, each slide moving along her tingling inner muscles. She attempted to squeeze him and prolong the wild feelings of each drive. As he stretched out over her, his large body shuddered, his heart pounded, as did hers.

He shifted backward onto his knees again, moved his hands to grip her hips. Pounding into her, he bit out almost angrily, "I crave your body. I cannot do without it. You cannot torture me like this again."

"Ohhhh, Thomas!" Her whole body squirmed against the bed. Fire, she felt like she was on fire, both inside and out. Her breaths were ragged. Her mind grew fuzzy. All she could think of was the wondrous rod driving into her. She thrust desperately back to meet him. "Ohhhh, ohhhh, ohhhh!"

She stopping moving, stopped breathing. He held still behind her as if he knew what would happen next. And then her juices flowed over him as he lay buried inside her. She moaned so deeply it felt like it came up from her toes. "Uhhhhh."

Clutching the pillow and fighting her way back to reality, she waited for her husband's mighty release, waited for his juices to flood within her. *This time, this time he will give me a babe. She was sure of it.*

Then while in the midst of a wild flurry of driving into her, while grunting in frantic need, he suddenly pulled out of her body. Before she could even cry out her complaint, his warm cream spurted over her bare bottom. It was such an odd feeling, his cream slowly dripping all over her cheeks and between her legs. But she didn't mind that. What she minded was not getting his seed poured within her.

"What do you, husband?" she craned her head around to gape at him. "You could have given me a babe!"

He scowled and immediately crawled off the bed, still breathing heavily. "I have already told you, I will *not* give you a babe. You must accept that, Gloriana." "Nay, I cannot." Tears streamed down her face as she sobbed in misery. She saw the tightness in his body; saw the way a vein pulsed in the side of his neck. She'd seen Geoffrey look this way too many times. Instinctively, she tensed, heart racing. She waited for Thomas to lose his temper, as Geoffrey would have when she dared to say anything he didn't want to hear. She waited for him to lean down and slap her.

He must have seen her fear because he growled several curses and then turned to walk away from her. His footsteps were so heavy that they sounded as if he stomped across the wooden floor. He went to the trunk and grabbed a rag, though she had no idea why.

His jaw was tight when he faced her again.

"I'm…I'm sorry," she apologized anxiously, hoping it would soothe his anger.

He blew out a breath as if he were trying to calm down. Yet as he walked back, it wasn't fury she saw in his eyes, it was sadness. She wanted to ask him about it, ask him to explain why he so fervently refused to even consider having another child. But she held her tongue. She was too emotional at the moment to try and talk logically. So she waited to see what her husband would do next.

He didn't say a word as he stopped beside the bed and leaned toward her with the rag. She stiffened in wariness. "Thomas?" "Lie still." She obeyed though her heart raced. To her surprise he gently wiped his cream from her buttocks and legs. It was such a tender act, so in contrast to the harsh words he'd spoken only moments ago.

"You will have my son to mother. That will have to be enough for you." He spoke quietly this time, his tone echoing with strain, with pain he carried and couldn't seem to share with her. He pulled her chemise down to cover her once more and finally admitted, "I *cannot* lose another wife in childbirth. I cannot."

Gloriana drew in a shaky breath and sat up, wiping at her tears. Frustration curled through her, for her longing for a babe, for Thomas and the pain he must have suffered. "Not all women die in childbirth, Thomas. I will *not* die giving birth."

Such horrible anguish filled his face as he looked at her that it pinched her heart. She recalled him telling her that he hadn't loved his first wife and that she hadn't loved him. He'd also told her that Sarah had died giving birth to James. When he'd spoken of this, she'd felt empathy for what he'd gone through, a bit of jealousy as well, although she'd felt too ashamed to even think about that. Sarah had died, but her child had lived. Thomas had a son, someone of his own blood, even though he'd apparently been away from James for most of his young life.

Now as she witnessed her strong, powerful husband standing before her with slumped shoulders and eyes downcast, she didn't know how to help him. She didn't know how to help *them* get through this difficult situation.

Finally he said flatly, "You cannot promise me that you won't die and I will not take the chance." Tears of frustration stung her eyes.

She wanted to grab him and shake him, make him let go of his fears. He wasn't being fair to her because of a tragedy in his past. But she sat there, clenching her fists in the fabric of her chemise, grimly holding onto the threads of her patience. She needed to think about the matter. She needed to find a way to reach him and help him heal. He found his braies and shoved them on, then his tunic and his boots. In seconds he was dressed and opening the door. He stood stiffly without looking back at her. "I do not wish to discuss this again, Gloriana."

She didn't say a word; just let him leave because she understood that was what he had to do for the moment. Part of her wanted to grieve for the loss of a babe she would never have. The stronger, determined part of her refused to give up yet. Geoffrey had nearly destroyed her. He'd beaten her, abused her in too many ways to consider. He'd battled down her love for life, her dreams. But even the short amount of time he'd been here, Thomas had saved her from despair and living her life in constant fear. She had to find a way to do the same for him. She had to help him let go of the fear of losing her in childbirth.

Her heart felt oddly lighter, her stomach fluttered with anticipation. She'd seen the hungry looks Thomas gave her. She'd experienced the depth of his need for her when they'd made love. He *cared* for her. Maybe he didn't love her, but he cared for her. Cared enough that he didn't want her to die and leave him. *He doesn't want to be left to raise another child on his own.* Nay, she refused to think that was all of it. Besides, he hadn't raised James. She lay back and thought upon the problem. *You were wrong, husband. We* will *talk of this again.*

***

Thomas strode down the stairs and into the great hall. It was still early and people were just beginning to awaken from where they slept on pallets over most of the hall's floor. The air was dank from sweaty bodies, slightly soiled rushes and the lack of air movement caused by the main door still being closed. He heard the cooks working in the kitchen and knew that soon the usual breads, cheeses, pastries and jugs of ale would be brought to the long tables soon to be set up. Before long everyone would be sitting down to break their morning's fast. His stomach felt tight, churned with tension. The thought of food didn't sit well with him. Not after what had happened in his bedchamber.

*Gloriana.* It sickened him that he'd hurt her. Her tears, the way her small shoulders had trembled from sobbing, had nearly done him in.

She'd let him do what he wanted to her, trusting him not to cause her pain, trusting him to give them both pleasure. He'd given her that. But when he'd reached his point of release, he'd pulled from her warm body to spill his seed.

He fisted his hands and ground his teeth to keep from roaring out his frustration. Everything had gotten crazy from that moment on. Her pain-filled cry of "You could have given me a babe!" still tortured him. His stern refusal haunted him as well.

A baby's cry on the far side of the great hall captured his attention. In the dim light of wall torches, he watched as a young mother pulled the baby to her and lowered her top enough that the youngling could latch onto her nipple. The babe couldn't be more than a few weeks old. Thomas stood there unable to look away, feeling gut-punched and as if he were bleeding on the inside. Tears stung his eyes.

Finally, he tore his gaze away. Sarah had never had the chance to nurse her son. Thomas had never gotten to see her act the happy, contented mother. It hurt. All of it. He'd been off battling in another senseless war. She'd taken a fall while his sister and Abernon were visiting and she'd gone into labor early. She'd given birth to his son while his sister and brother-in-law were there for her. They'd been helpless to save her life. But James had lived. He thanked God every day for that. Still, the guilt of not being there for Sarah weighed so heavily on him that at times he couldn't breathe from it. Along with that, he bore the guilt for not having been a better husband...for not having loved her.

A young blonde maid bustled by him headed for the kitchen and his thoughts turned to Gloriana. He didn't understand his feelings for her yet, but they were strong. What he did know was that he *could not* lose her. Her vow that she wouldn't die giving birth were foolish words. Many women bled to death in childbirth. *But many more don't.*

He closed his eyes on a wave of wrenching pain. Sarah had wanted a child. He'd given it to her. He couldn't help feeling that he'd been at fault for her death. He *would not* risk Gloriana's life that way!

Gerald walked up to him, pulling Thomas from his troubled musings. The bailiff's face was covered by the scraggly start of a beard over his tight jaw. His eyes narrowed. "What upsets you, Lord Middlemound?" He glanced toward a pair of soldiers grumbling testily as they rose from their pallets nearby, then he lowered his tone. "Do you worry because you have not heard back from the message sent to Lord Abernon? I can send another group of soldiers out."

"It concerns me, but, nay, we will wait another day or two." Thomas hoped with his answer that the other man would simply walk away.

Instead Gerald's gaze darted toward the stairs and his frown became darker. "Is Lady Gloriana all right?"

He was getting tired of not being trusted with her. He straightened his shoulders and flexed his hands at his sides in irritation. "She is not happy with me. Tis a private matter."

Then he looked more closely at the older man, saw the concern in his eyes when their gazes met. The man was protective of Gloriana and still unsure of their marriage. He knew much of her history with Geoffrey and didn't want to see her suffer again. He could not fault the warrior for that.

Gerald's expression remained hard. "Do *not* hurt her."

Even if Thomas understood Gerald's worry, he was in a foul mood. He was spoiling for a fight, something physical to release the tension curling within him. He stepped nearly nose-to-nose with the man of similar height and build. "I will not hurt her! And I refuse to continue to reassure you, or anyone else, about the matter." Gerald's nostrils flared, but he didn't make a move. Their silent testing each other now drew the attention of many of the nearby people. It was a bad situation. Yet Thomas wouldn't be the first to back down. The man owed him respect as his lord.

From the corner of his eye, Thomas saw Rowan walk out of the kitchen nibbling on a chunk of bread.

As soon as Rowan turned and glanced in their direction, he strode toward them. "What goes on here?" Rowan demanded, standing next to Thomas in support. Gerald sent him a do-not-interfere look, though he remained quiet.

"Nothing, Sir Rowan," Thomas bit out. His gaze settled on the bailiff again, anger sizzling just below the surface.

Thomas raised his gaze to take in the uneasy soldiers and servants close to them, watching, waiting. A tense silence filled the area. He did not like having to defend himself. He raised his voice so all in the hall could hear him. "This is the *last* time I will tell you all that I will never hurt your lady. I am *not* Geoffrey Stewart. I will never raise my hand to my wife."

Some of the tension eased, but he knew they were all aware that

Stewart had done more than beat Gloriana. He blew out a frustrated breath. "We may argue from time to time, like all couples. But I will never verbally abuse my wife, either." Deciding that he'd said more than enough, Thomas moved around Gerald, shooting warning looks at everyone he passed as he hurried toward the keep's door. He prayed he'd hear from Abernon this day before his mood turned even worse. He wanted his son with him, needed a chance to right the wrongs he'd done James. Most of all he wanted to be alone to get over his anger with Gloriana.

But Rowan was on his heels when he walked out onto the steps. In truth, Rowan's presence was the only one he truly didn't mind. His friend had a way of settling him down. Just as Thomas knew how to calm Rowan when the troubles in his past came back to haunt him.

***

Rowan studied Thomas's stiff posture, the rigid muscles of his chest. He feared that as upset as his friend was, Gloriana was even more distressed. Thomas's emotions ran deep, though he usually kept them hidden. That Thomas had nearly gone to blows in the hall with Gerald was a clear sign that he had taken about as much as he could handle. He knew Thomas hadn't minded taking on this large holding, although he knew Thomas had known getting the people here to accept him would be difficult. Such was always the case when a new lord took over a holding. Being ordered to marry the previous lord's widow hadn't been something Thomas had wanted. As always, he'd obeyed his King, done his duty. Marrying Gloriana hadn't been such a hardship—even Rowan, a man who'd never before wanted marriage, wouldn't have found being her husband a hardship. No, he knew that for the most part Thomas was happy in the marriage. Except for this business about Gloriana wanting a baby and him being unable to give her one.

"Tis a bad situation," Thomas finally said, looking up at the guard walking on the parapet.

Rowan took a deep breath. The matter was a prickly one and his loyalties were strained. He had strong feelings for Gloriana and didn't want to see her hurt in any way. But his feelings for Thomas were intense as well. He needed to choose his words carefully. "For both of you, aye. I know your fears, and I know how strongly

Gloriana wants a babe of her own." He'd seen the joy that crossed her face when the castle's children came around her. She drew them like flies to crumbs. Her eyes danced with delight when they were nearby.

Her smile was never bigger.

He saw the pain that washed over Thomas's face, but he had to say more. "You're hurting her with your stubbornness. Driving her away."

Thomas reached up to run a hand through his hair, a habit Rowan knew he had when frustrated. The day was breezy and fluttered his hair around his face. "She needs to accept my decision."

"You fought about this, didn't you?"

"Aye. After..." Thomas grimaced as he looked at Rowan before focusing across the bailey again. Rowan sniffed and inhaled the scent of the aftereffects of lovemaking. Envy curled through him. Longing. "After you returned to her bed this morn. After you made love to her," he said the words dully.

Thomas nodded and continued looking away.

Rowan sensed his friend felt guilt about the matter, which was foolish. Thomas and Gloriana were married. Having sexual relations was to be expected. Truly Rowan was all right with that, but he needed, *wanted* intimacy with Thomas as well. He'd known Thomas had not slept in his marital bedchamber these past few nights, but he'd not come to Rowan's bed, either. He could have found the chamber Thomas slept in and gone to him, but he'd decided to wait for his lover to approach him. Now he was sexually frustrated. Standing here next to the man who could take care of that matter was difficult. His cock throbbed with an aching need for release. He wanted to find a place of privacy and bend Thomas over, drive into his ass. Appease his desire and take some of the tension off Thomas as well.

Instead he fought back all of it and focused on the problem of Gloriana. "She didn't want your special tea this time, I take it."

Thomas's shoulders stiffened. "I did not try to give her any." He drew in a deep breath and blew it out. "This morn I used another method. I withdrew from her body before shooting my seed."

"God's teeth!" Rowan snapped in disgust. "Twould be kinder if you just didn't have sex with her."

"Kinder, but impossible. My body craves hers." Thomas faced Rowan, clearly frustrated. He lowered his tone, "Just as I crave yours."

The heat in Thomas's eyes, the nearness, the intense awareness for one another was nearly Rowan's undoing. He desperately wanted to pull Thomas to him. He wanted to plant his lips against Thomas's. He wanted to reach down and grab Thomas's cock. He wanted Thomas to grab his as well. His body thrummed with a powerful need that couldn't be satisfied. At least not now.

His gaze softened, but his lowered tone hardened, "Come to me this night."

Several men walked from the keep behind them, gave them a curious look. Thomas gave a curt nod.

"As we discussed, I will talk to Gerald about sending more men out on the morrow," Rowan said. He and Thomas had already talked about the subject yesterday. The first group of men sent with a message should have been back by now, unless Abernon had delayed in taking his time to prepare a response.

"Aye, do so." Thomas headed for the paddocks, calling over his shoulder to the men who had just passed. "I will ride into the village now. You three, prepare to ride with me."

***

Gloriana stood at the window of their bedchamber and watched her husband ride away from the castle with three of his men. She had no idea where he was headed this day. She doubted it was farther than the village since he had taken so few men with him. Neither Sir Gerald nor Rowan accompanied him, which puzzled her a bit, but also made her believe whatever mission he was off on wasn't serious.

She was worried about him. He could be so impossibly stubborn at times that she just wanted to grab hold of him and shake some sense into him. *What a bizarre image, that.* He towered over her by a foot, out muscled her by a lot. In physical comparison, she was that tiny woman he believed her to be. Yet she was finding herself to be stronger in spirit with every passing day. Thomas didn't terrorize her, didn't try to demean her, didn't attempt to lower her in everyone's eyes the way Geoffrey had. He allowed her to fulfill her role as chatelaine, though she knew he watched from a distance. He listened to her occasional chatter about this or that matter to do with running the keep. He allowed her to be what she wanted to be…except a mother to his babe. Oh, he wanted her to act as a mother to his son when he came here, if he came here, which she gladly would do. But the man refused to listen to reason about giving her a babe.

*Stubborn, stubborn man!* All right, she was being particularly stubborn about wanting a babe born of her body as well. But she longed to hold a baby close and smooth her hand over its downy-covered head. She yearned to inhale a baby's sweet scent, watch it smile up at her. Smile up at her with Thomas's eyes.

*Thomas.* Such complicated feelings she had for her warrior husband. Her woman's place quivered, and she recognized what wonders it had felt earlier. He'd taken her body with such raw passion, such desperate need. He'd forced her to cry out as everything in her had exploded. And then he'd pulled from her body at the longed-for moment. He'd robbed her of the chance to have a baby. His words had been even crueler.

Tears misted her eyes even as anger at his stubbornness spread within her. *Obstinate man!* He had won this round of what had become an important battle. But she would not give up, could not give up.

***

The great hall echoed with so much noise that Thomas's head throbbed from it. His mood had soured as the day went on. The argument, brief as it was, with Gloriana had stayed at the forefront of his thoughts all day. Every time he closed his eyes for even a second, he'd seen the tears on her gentle face, heard the anguish in her sobs. How many times had his attention wandered from what he'd been doing to wondering if he truly was wrong about the babe? How many times had he then remembered being told how Sarah had bled to death giving birth to James? He did not even want to think about such a situation with Gloriana. And yet seeing and hearing her misery…

He heard her gentle laugh as she shared something of her day with Rowan, who tonight sat beside her and not him. He wanted to hear that sound for the rest of his days.

"Tis good to hear you laugh, wife," he said, surprising himself.

Both Gloriana and Rowan looked curiously at him, making him feel foolish. Surprising him even more since they'd barely spoken since his return a couple of hours ago, she gave him a gentle smile. "Twould be good to hear *you* laugh, my lord."

"I've had nothing to laugh at of late." Not wanting to see pity in her eyes, he concentrated on the trencher of venison stew in front of him.

"Mayhap we should have a band of minstrels come here to entertain before long. Twould lighten everyone's mood." She offered the suggestion with clear hope in her voice. Rowan said gently, "I'm afraid, my lady, that your husband is not fond of traveling minstrels."

"Oh, that's too bad. I'd hoped… Well, never mind. It was a foolish idea anyway." She picked up her cup of mead and sipped at it.

His friend was right; Thomas didn't particularly enjoy the silly dancing about and endless nonsense of the jokers who came with the traveling minstrels. And he wasn't fond of minstrels by themselves. Yet at the way her small shoulders slumped, he said, "Arrange for a group to come to Middlemound; preferably in a fortnight." The smile she flashed him stole deep into his heart. Such a small concession had greatly pleased her. He drew in a calmer breath, the heaviness that had been inside him all day lifted. All because of her gentle smile.

The main door grated open and drew his attention, as well as that of Rowan and many of the men nearby. He tensed, watching the men he'd sent to Abernon walk into the hall. The lead soldier strode straight to Thomas with a rolled parchment.

"Lord Abernon took longer than we'd expected to write out a response, my lord. We returned as quickly as we could." He handed over the missive and then went to find a seat at one of the tables to take his sup with the men who had ridden with him.

Thomas's palms were sweating. He was almost afraid to look at the message. From the corner of his eye, he noted how Rowan, too, had stiffened, as had Gloriana, whose brow had furrowed in concern.

Fearing he wouldn't like what was written and would say something he shouldn't in front of the men about the hall all looking curiously at him, he shoved back his chair. "I will read this in the solar. Rowan, join me."

Gloriana blinked at him with a wounded look in her eyes. She needed to know what was in the message too, but he preferred to read the news alone first. Well, alone with Rowan. Then he realized what a ridiculous thought that was. Still, he would stand behind his decision. "I will talk with you later about the message," he said with less force.

As they walked upstairs, Rowan said under his breath, "She should have been included in this matter. You've hurt her yet again." Thomas scowled back at Rowan, who merely narrowed his eyes in return. He strode down the hallway to the solar. "If this is bad news, I need time to come to terms with it. I refuse to show weakness in front of my wife."

Rowan snorted. "Yet you have no problem with showing it in front of me." Thomas chose not to respond because what his lover had said was true. But then they'd been through so much together. He trusted that Rowan would not betray him in any manner, as he would not betray Rowan.

The instant Thomas closed the door behind them, he began untying and unrolling the parchment. His stomach knotted. He read over the brief message and then the paper crinkled as he crushed it in his hands. He knew fury sparked in his eyes when his gaze lifted to Rowan.

"As I suspected, Abernon does not wish to turn over my son." Thomas thought again about what he'd read. "But Abernon will discuss the matter further…at his castle. I am to come there, with Gloriana." He met and held Rowan's gaze. "With *you* as well."

Rowan's eyes narrowed, his brow furrowed. "You think he suspects…"

Thomas shrugged. "Nothing was said in written words, but, aye, I suspect he knows. How, I do not know."

He had no idea how Abernon would know about his personal relationship with Rowan. Abernon hadn't flat-out said anything in the missive. But Thomas felt in his gut that his brother-in-law had his suspicions. What he and Rowan had wasn't sick or twisted, as Abernon might think. They truly cared about each other and that caring went far beyond their sharing intense passion. He would defend their bond with his life if necessary. And he would not be denied his son because of it!

He paced over to the window to look outside. His mind was in as much turmoil as the clouds moving darkly overhead. Everything in his life at the moment was a struggle. His issues with Gloriana. His relationship with Rowan. His determination to get his son back. He would deal with matters one problem at a time.

"We ride to Abernon on the morrow." He would confront his brother-in-law first.

***

Gloriana paced the semi-darkness of her bedchamber, lit only by the two candles on bedside tables. The keep was silent. Soldiers preparing to leave at first light had bedded down early. Everyone else would probably rest anxiously tonight, none knowing whether the men were riding into a battle and an eventual attempt to lay siege to Abernon. She, too, was distressed, uncertain. When Thomas had told her the news not long after talking alone with Rowan, he'd been a troubled man. He didn't want to bring a battle to his sister's home, but he wanted his son. And she'd sensed there was trouble that involved Rowan as well. Something in the way he kept looking at his friend. There'd been such frustration in his eyes, such anger, and such determination. Rowan, too, had appeared upset. The concern in his expressive eyes was more intense than normal. She worried about them both. She faced the rumpled bed where she'd tossed and turned until she couldn't stay there another second. Thomas had not yet come to bed...at least not to their marital bed. Her men—and, yes, she thought of them both as *her* men—were deeply troubled this night. They needed each other at such times, which she truly didn't mind. But she needed reassuring, too. She needed the warmth of Thomas's body next to hers, *in* hers. She needed to comfort him and make him believe that everything would be all right, even if she only hoped it would be. She needed to reassure Rowan, too.

Heart racing, she straightened her shoulders, and walked quietly out of her room. With each step down the long hallway in bare feet, she prayed she wasn't making a mistake. She'd seen them together once before and the memory of it still gave her wicked fantasies. Thomas had reluctantly talked about their relationship, seemed pleased it didn't repulse her. She was certain he'd talked about the awkward conversation with Rowan. But would they be upset with her coming to see them now? Would they be angered if she walked in on them as they...as they "fucked"?

She could turn back to her bedchamber—probably should—but instead she continued toward Rowan's chamber door. Her hand shook as she started to knock. When she heard soft moans, she dropped her hand. *This is private! Turn away.*

Yet as the moans continued, she found her hand carefully opening the door a crack. Her heart pounded so loudly she hoped they couldn't hear her as she peeked into the candle-lit room. She gaped, not in horror but in fascination. Thomas and Rowan stood naked by the bed, and she was certain she'd never seen such a wondrous sight. Two extremely well-toned men, tall with long, muscled legs, both with many battle scars, and so very, very handsome.

She felt a fluttering of excitement low in her body. As she wondered at it, she watched Thomas reach up to caress Rowan's lower lip with a finger. Rowan's eyes heated and then he drew the finger into his mouth for but a second. His chest swelled and shuddered when Thomas inched closer. Then he wrapped his powerful arms around Thomas and tugged him even closer, so close their bodies were aligned so that their cocks rubbed together.

Gloriana trembled all over, watching, aching to be a part of what they were doing. She wanted to feel Thomas's finger trace over her lips, wanted to suck on it just as Rowan had done. She wanted to feel Rowan's arms around her. She wanted to stand between their bodies, feel both of their cocks rubbing against her. *Such wicked, wicked thoughts!* Moisture beaded between her shaking legs. She could not look away from the two lovers.

And then Rowan kissed Thomas, gently, in striking contrast to the hardened warrior he was. His mouth slanted over Thomas's, his tongue slid slowly along the crease of Thomas's lips. The muscles in his back rippled as he seemed to fight deepening the kiss too soon.

Gloriana pressed a hand to her envious lips. To be kissed so tenderly… Then she remembered Thomas kissing her with gentleness, too. She smiled at the memory.

But Thomas had clearly tired of going slow, and she watched him enfold Rowan in his powerful embrace. His lower body moved against Rowan while his mouth took everything Rowan had to give. Gloriana wanted *this* kind of kiss! Gentleness was nice, but *this*…this kiss had her heart racing, had heat swirling all through her. She stamped her foot in irritation.

That small noise drew their attention, or at least their gazes. She had the feeling they'd both known she was there watching them. They didn't move apart, their bodies still aligned, cocks still touching. But Rowan's eyes mirrored amusement at her sudden mortification at having been caught watching something she shouldn't have been observing.

It was Thomas who sighed in resignation and motioned her into the chamber. "I see that your curiosity has gotten the better of you, Glori. Come in and close the door."

Her face flamed, but she raised her chin as she obeyed.

"Twas not curiosity that brought me here, my lord. I wish to be held and comforted this night as well." It was curiosity that had kept her watching them, intrigued and feeling left out.

"Tis more than simple 'comforting' I need. My frustrations run high at the moment." He looked directly at her. "My needs are intense. I fear I wouldn't have been gentle enough with you tonight."

Gloriana was still quivering inside, still thinking about what she'd witnessed. And with the two men continuing to stand with their aroused bodies touching one another, she couldn't stand idly by any longer. She blew out a breath of exasperation. "Mayhap we can all get what we desire."

Rowan's lips twitched in amusement. Thomas looked uncertain.

She'd hoped they would just understand what she meant without having to explain this lust she felt. She heaved a sigh and focused on Thomas. "You can satisfy your great needs with Rowan, as he can with you. I'm fine with that." When they both still watched her in silence, she put her hands on hips and said pointedly, "But I insist on one…or both of you…satisfying me as well. Mayhap a bit more gently." Her face flamed at her bold statement, but she refused to take it back.

In truth, the idea of both of them touching her, making love to her was making her a bit light-headed with desire.

When they both raised eyebrows, she ignored the nervous tingling in her stomach and added with determination, "And I insist on being allowed to give comfort to each of you."

"Give 'comfort'?" Thomas asked, his tone confused.

"Reassurance. Hugging. Touching gently, as the two of you were doing moments ago. I want to give that." She drew in a breath and lifted her chin. "I want it as well."

Rowan's grin tipped up one side of his tempting mouth, heat flared in his eyes. He looked toward Thomas clearly intending to see how his friend answered. Thomas's brow had creased and he appeared unsure of how to respond.

Annoyed with her husband's lack of response, she decided to take action. She walked to them, noticing how they both tensed, seemed to hold each other tighter in their uncertainty. She would not back down now.

Drawing on her strength of will, she stopped next to them in her thin cotton chemise. Thomas's eyes widened at her daring. And then she wrapped her arms around the two of them as much as she could. She settled her face to where their chests touched and breathed out a sigh of contentment. It felt so right, being here with the men that had become so important to her. She gave them a tiny squeeze as best she could.

Rowan immediately relaxed and gave her the top of her head a gentle kiss. Yet he said nothing, waiting for Thomas's reaction.

She held her breath, worried that she'd made a fool of herself.

Worried that Thomas would now turn her away, force her to leave them. Then she felt the tension leave his big body and heard his sigh of resignation.

Impatient that he hadn't actually spoken yet, she kissed Thomas's bare chest and then turned to kiss Rowan's. Then she looked up expectantly at them both. "Well?"

"Tis your wife, my friend. What say you?" Rowan slid a hand around her back, toyed with the end of her long braid. "I'm willing."

Thomas was silent for several seconds, although his gaze had heated, his nostrils flared. She could tell he was thinking it over, studying his lover, worrying about her. So many emotions crossed over his dear, handsome face. She saw surprise and interest, concern and acceptance, even a brief flash of jealousy, but she wasn't sure of whom it was about: her or Rowan. She couldn't take much more of his indecision. Finally he nodded. "I will not see you hurt in this, Glori. All the more intense loving will be between Rowan and me. Understand?"

She smiled. Her whole body sizzled with excitement. In her delight, she devilishly reached out and lightly pinched each of their bare butts.

## Chapter Seven

"Glori!" Thomas looked down at her, saw the teasing grin on her face, and knew he was lost.

Rowan chortled. "You're asking for trouble, my lady." But his gaze held warmth as he pinched her bottom in return before edging away from Thomas and Gloriana. Thomas frowned at Rowan's action and then calmed. If he were agreeing to this arrangement, then he had to accept that his weren't the only hands that would touch his wife's body. His weren't the only lips that would taste of her sweetness. Another brief twinge of jealousy sparked, but he tamped it down. He trusted Rowan with his life, with loving him. He would trust Rowan not to hurt Gloriana.

She giggled in delight and scooted back several feet, pulling Thomas from his musings. Her face grew pink, but she reached for the hem of her chemise. His heart pounded as he watched mesmerized as she uncovered herself. She had such a perfect body. He vividly recalled each and every inch of it. He knew her scent, knew her softness. His cock grew to the point of aching. He wanted her.

He felt a twinge of possessiveness, but then he glanced toward an equally naked Rowan and experienced the same possessiveness toward him. He wanted them both.

She was blushing all over, yet she stood waiting for their further reaction. Thomas gave her a smile of approval.

In return, she lowered her eyes for a second before saying, "I feel truly blessed to be here with two such handsome men. To soon share something very special with you both."

Thomas reached out to gently touch the side of her face. He didn't speak; couldn't seem to find the right words to say, but he hoped she understood how special a moment this was for him as well.

Rowan wasn't nearly as tongue-tied as he. He looked from Gloriana to Thomas and said, "Tis we, dear Glori, who are blessed."

Thomas nodded in agreement. This small woman had suffered much in her previous marriage, had at first been wary of him, and now she was ready to try something completely foreign to her…to him as well. He'd never made love with another man and a woman at the same time. It both excited him and worried him.

"As much as I want this, I know not how to go about it," Thomas said quietly. He didn't want to fail either of them. What he did know was that his erection had grown even harder since his wife had shed her garment. "I refuse to have you hurt."

He reached down and stroked the length of his cock, pleased to see her eyes widen as she watched him. Rowan observed him, too, but right now he was more interested in Gloriana's reaction. He stroked his rod again, slower, thumbing the head. Her breasts rose and fell, and she couldn't seem to look away from what he was doing.

Thomas watched her swallow hard while he stroked his throbbing cock yet another time. He saw her tremble. Her responses greatly pleased him. He imagined if he looked between her legs, he would find moisture beading there. Just the thought of that made him even more desperate for their lovemaking.

Then Rowan, too, wrapped a hand around his hardened rod. Gloriana shifted her focus and breathed shakily as she watched him move his hand up and down the shaft. Thomas watched as well, aching to touch that cock, to feel it rammed into him or take it in his mouth. Even more, he fought an almost violent urge to bend Rowan over and drive into his tight hole. Right here in front of his wife.

Rowan met his eyes and gave him a look of understanding. "I know, my friend. My need is mighty, too." Rowan rubbed his cock once more, his chest shuddering. "I hadn't thought you were experienced with a ménage a trois. I am, though I've not done this very often."

***

Watching the two massive men each stroking their swollen rods had Gloriana trembling from nose to toe. She wanted to touch each of those shafts. She wanted to feel them inside her. Separately. Together. She had such a powerful ache within her.

"I fear I can't be gentle right now." Thomas's expression was tense as he looked to her. "I want you too much. I want Rowan too much."

A glance at Rowan and she knew he felt the same heated desire. Both men needed the release they'd prepared to seek before she'd interrupted them. In truth, she wished to observe their union and sate her curiosity almost as much as she wanted fulfillment herself.

"I cannot watch the two of you suffering so. Do whatever you need to do." She went over to sit on the rumpled bed to watch. "Mayhap when you're finished..."

"Nay, we can all be satisfied together," Rowan protested. "I will feast on your sweetness." He looked toward Thomas. "You will take my ass."

*Feast on her sweetness?* Gloriana quivered in anticipation. *Did he mean like...* She felt heat climbing up her face as she remembered Thomas spreading her legs one time and putting his mouth upon her woman's place. Her pulse raced and moisture beaded at her lower lips. Then she looked to Thomas, worried about his feelings toward what Rowan had said. Would he let his friend touch her in such a way?

Thomas had a small frown on his brow, but he didn't voice disapproval. She needed an answer to her concern. "Do you agree with this, my lord?" She wanted this 'feasting,' but not if her husband was unhappy with it.

Thomas frowned for a second and then nodded. "If I had the patience right now, I would do it. But my need to deliver a pounding is too fierce." He stroked his swollen shaft steadily, looked with urgency at his friend. "Lie on your back, Glori, toward the middle of the bed. Spread your legs wide."

Heart racing but eager to obey, she quickly scrambled back into the position requested. She was nervous feeling so exposed, so vulnerable. But seeing both men watching her so ardently, seeing both draw in a deep breath pleased her. Because of their clear approval, she relaxed. She was seeing them at their most vulnerable as well.

Rowan had been pulling harder, faster, on his swollen cock while she moved on his bed. He grew still and she watched in wonder as a thin cream flowed over his hand. Then tension eased from his face. He turned to Thomas, who took some of the cream and coated his long shaft with it. The action made her lower lips pulse, made her ache with longing. What a waste it seemed, using Rowan's essence in such a manner. He could have possibly given a woman a babe...given *her* a babe. She would have gladly borne him a child, though she really wished to have one with Thomas. Now she felt ashamed for having such thoughts about the man who wasn't her husband.

Thomas caught her sad look, and she noted how his eyes were dark with shadows. *Pain? Regret? Guilt for his decision not to get her with child?* She truly didn't want to give him more burdens to bear, yet she so desperately wanted a baby. But she would settle for mothering his son if that was her only choice. Yet, even thinking that, she wasn't ready to completely give up on him changing his mind.

He heaved a sigh, "Do not think about it now. I cannot think about it."

Rowan clearly knew what they were discussing, although she wasn't exactly sure what Thomas had meant. She was distracted, though, when Rowan moved toward the bed. Shivers swept over her, and she looked anxiously up at Thomas. *Was he really all right with this?*

Thomas's expression was hard to read. His jaw appeared tight; his hands were fisted at his sides. But he gave her a curt nod.

She returned her focus to Rowan as he bent down over the end and looked at her intently. "Think only of me, my lady. Of how I'm going to put my mouth against your body. Of how I'm going to put my tongue inside and taste of your sweet nectar."

Her eyes widened at his husky words. *His mouth to her? His tongue inside her?* Every inch of her body felt alive with anticipation. More so as he put his large hands to her legs and carefully pushed them back until her heels rested on the bed. She breathed rapidly, nervous again. Then he shifted forward until his shoulders touched the backs of her thighs. His head rested only inches above the hairy patch between her legs. She felt his warm breath on her. Her stomach tightened. Her heartbeat pounded until it sounded loud in her ears.

He gripped her sides, and then turned his hungry gaze back to Thomas. "I am ready, my lord," he gritted out.

*Thomas!* How could she have forgotten her husband? True, she was most curious, most eager for what Rowan intended to do to her. *Put his mouth to her. His tongue inside her.* But she could not find any kind of pleasure unless Thomas did as well! He stood near the end of the bed, behind his lover, still rubbing his thick cock. His expression was tight with strain.

"Husband, I cannot see you suffering so. Do what you need. Rowan says he is ready," she pleaded. Thomas blinked at her and then gave a small smile. He bent down and reached around Rowan before straightening with more of the other man's cream on his fingers. He held her gaze, appearing somewhat amused by her insistence. "Rowan is almost ready, wife," he corrected her. He reached down to put one coated finger to Rowan's ass.

Curiosity was killing her. Annoyed at not being able to see what he was doing, she shifted up to brace her body on her elbows so that she could watch. Both men gave her amused looks.

"Our Lady Gloriana is a very curious woman." Rowan smiled at her, looking pleased. Then he tensed, his face tight, his shoulders taut. He drew in a breath.

She glanced to Thomas as he focused on Rowan and began gently sliding his finger into the other man's body. Then as Rowan's chest sucked in with a deep inhale, Thomas quickly added a second finger. An action which made Rowan's lips grow thin and his nostrils flare. *Was he in pain?* She couldn't bear the idea. "You're hurting him!" she accused Thomas, wanting him to stop immediately.

Thomas froze, although he didn't remove his fingers from Rowan's body. It was Rowan who blew out a breath and then gritted out, "Nay, he is not." He pressed his body back against Thomas's hand. "He is preparing me to accept his cock."

"Oh." Gloriana remembered how Thomas had "prepared" her before he drove into her body. She'd been wary at first, but what he'd done had indeed gotten her ready for his large cock. "I…I understand."

Thomas appeared relieved that she no longer worried as much. She studied the two men as Thomas carefully moved his fingers in and out of Rowan's small hole, as he watched her. She liked how he included her in this, liked how he had been concerned at her accusation. She should have known he would never hurt Rowan.

She turned her focus to Rowan, who grimaced and dragged in shuddering breaths, but he made no attempts to make Thomas stop what he was doing. She wondered what he felt, wondered what it would feel like having fingers shoved into her puckered hole. No doubt she would be squirming and grimacing, too. Yet they were to do more than this. Obviously much was needed to be done to get Rowan's body ready to accept such an invasion.

Gloriana found herself saying sympathetically, "This preparing is good."

Rowan gasped, "Aye, tis very good." He turned his head toward Thomas. "Tis ready I am. Now."

He was ready? *Was she?* She tensed, waiting, worrying.

Thomas moved directly behind Rowan, holding his long, thick cock in his hand. He pressed the broad head against Rowan's small opening. *How could it possibly go in?* She worried her lower lip, frowning in distress.

"It will be all right, Glori," Rowan husked out. He drew her gaze, and she saw how he gritted his teeth together. "Do not worry."

But she held her breath and worried for him anyway. How could she not?

"I would not hurt him," Thomas confirmed and now she looked to him.

Her husband, too, ground his teeth together. He slipped the head of his cock inside Rowan's body. His face tightened in strain as he held still, letting Rowan adjust to him. Much like he'd done with her, letting her body adjust to his fullness.

"More," Rowan ordered gruffly, pushing backward.

Thomas pushed his rod farther into Rowan's body a little at a time. She watched Rowan draw in a deep breath, saw him stiffen. She could only imagine what he was feeling. Thomas was very well endowed, but then so was Rowan. Then she remembered her husband coming home that one night in pain. Rowan had driven his shaft into Thomas that time. "Pounded" Thomas had said. "Ridden him hard." What they did to one another caused pain, but obviously it did more than that.

She watched in worried fascination as Thomas's breaths blew out in short bursts as he pulled nearly out of his lover's small hole before pushing even father back inside. He repeated the actions until his entire shaft had disappeared.

Both men held still for several seconds, both were breathing hard. She fretted over both of them.

Finally some of the tension eased from Rowan's face. He captured her gaze and his eyes were heated. "Lie back, sweet Glori." She looked to where Thomas held Rowan's hips, holding his cock deep inside the other man's body. Surely Rowan couldn't feast on her now while Thomas was...

Thomas gave her a reassuring glance. "You will do as he says."

Trembling with anticipation and thrumming with excitement at watching her two special men, she lay back. Rowan immediately gripped her sides once more and lowered his head. His tongue darted out and trailed slowly over her swollen lips, making her jerk, making her gasp, "Oh! Oh my!" She saw Thomas tighten his hold on Rowan, saw him pull back and drive deep. She could almost feel the near-pain as Rowan sucked in a breath and froze.

And then he blew out a breath and thrust his tongue into her body. She arched upward, shoving at him, gasping in wonder. Every inch of her body seemed to tingle, to want more, so much more. She clutched at the linen beneath her.

Time and again she watched Thomas drive in and out of Rowan's body. His beard-stubbled jaw clenched. His breaths became ragged.

Over and over Rowan grimaced, shoved backward to demand more. He panted harder each time.

Yet Rowan did not ignore her needs to satisfy his own. He found her sensitized bud and nibbled on it, making her let go of the bed linen and clutch at his head. "Oh! Oh! Yes!"

He drove his tongue into her, plunging deep, making her squirm. "Oh, Rowan!" She panted, whimpered. He tortured her with pleasure until she bucked wildly against his mouth. "Ohhhh. Ohhh. Oh. My. God!" Her juices flowed freely and she collapsed against the mattress.

Gloriana was lost in the wonder of it all when she watched Thomas give a final thrust of his hips.

Rowan arched down into the bed. He grimaced in strain, holding his breath. Behind him Thomas gave a guttural cry and filled Rowan's body with streams of white cream. Again, she was saddened at the thought that if he'd flooded into *her* body, he might have gotten her with child.

Jarring her from her depression, both men slumped together on the end of the bed. She would not focus on the other matter now. She still clung to hope that she could change Thomas's mind. Just as she thought all was over, Thomas stood. Rowan shifted to sit on the end of the bed with his cock stabbing the air, swollen and needing release. Her husband moved to his knees and without hesitation took Rowan's cock into his mouth. He worked it, sucking on it in the same way she'd seen Rowan do to Thomas nearly two weeks ago.

She was fascinated at the pleasure she saw on both men's faces. A tingling returned to her stomach, then to her woman's place. Desire. She wanted to know the kind of pleasure they were sharing. One day she wanted to take Thomas's shaft into her mouth, suckle on it the way he was doing with Rowan. And she wanted to do the same with Rowan. What would her husband feel when he watched her take his lover's cock into her mouth? Would it excite him as much as watching Thomas savor

Rowan's rod excited her?

When Rowan was finally sated, Thomas stood again and looked warily at her. "What think you, my lady?"

Gloriana smiled at each man, more so at Thomas. "I thank you both for sharing this with me. Twas very special."

Rowan grinned as Thomas sighed in relief. "Twill be even better next time, sweet Glori."

Heart racing, she looked to her husband. "Next time?"

He nodded. "If you wish, my wife." His expression turned serious. "Now, tis time we returned to our own chamber. We all need what rest we can get, for the morrow promises to be difficult. We leave for Abernon at dawn."

***

It took them two days to reach Montrose Castle. By the time Thomas led Gloriana, Rowan and twenty of his soldiers into the main bailey late in the afternoon, he felt weary to the bone. He knew the others in their party were equally tired. He'd forced them to make this first part of their trip to Abernon at a brisk pace. The weather had been unusually cold for this early in the fall, so no one had protested riding faster. Even now gray clouds roiled overhead with the threat of rain. He'd expected it before now; was grateful they'd made it here before the rain started. Rain would slow their trip, but he'd needed to stop here to take care of Montrose matters. He reined in just inside the main gate and glanced back at Gloriana.

Her small form was buried within a velvet fur-lined cloak with a hood. He watched her shiver against the cold; saw how pale and drawn what little of her face he could see appeared. Yet she'd not complained once. He owed her much for making this journey, for supporting him in his quest to get James.

"We must get you into the keep, wife. Get you before a warm fire." He blinked in annoyance as a drop of rain touched his face. He looked toward his first knight. "Rowan, see to Gloriana. I must talk to Sir Richard for a moment before joining you." With a nod of agreement, Rowan dismounted and then lifted her to the ground as well. A light rain started falling. His arm swept around her shoulders and he hurried her toward the three-story, square stone building in the center of the castle's grounds. Thomas watched them go and was at ease. His friend would take good care of her, just as he'd done during the ride here. Thomas's thoughts had been too focused on getting to Abernon and claiming his son. He should have paid more attention to Gloriana. He would find a way to make up for his neglect of her.

Sir Richard Compton, his bailiff here, walked toward him from where he'd been talking to several of the guards by the gatehouse. "My lord, welcome back to Montrose. It has been too long since we've seen you here. There's much to discuss."

Thomas had feared as much, yet he would not stay more than a day… unless the weather caused an even longer delay. The light rain was quickly becoming heavier. He knew the men behind him were anxious to get out of it as much as he. "I'll talk with you in the solar after you see that these men are taken care of."

He dismounted and handed his reins to a young page who ran up, looking eager to be of help. Then he strode toward the keep. What he really wanted now was hot food, cold ale, dry clothes, and his wife. Not particularly in that order. His hunger for Gloriana had gained strength since they'd last made love two nights ago. He'd left Rowan's chamber sated, far less stressed, surprised and pleased by what the three of them had done. But he'd still been determined to see his precious Glori satisfied as well. Back in their own bedchamber, she'd been greedy in her demands of him. His shy bride was quickly changing, becoming more confident in herself and what she wanted, for which he was glad. His sexual needs were mighty, as were Rowan's. It appeared that Glori's were as well.

Striding through the rain, he replayed the heated time between him and Glori. He'd nearly lost all control. He'd pulled from her body almost too late. He'd spilled some of his seed inside her, though most of it had been shot over her soft stomach. She'd been so upset with him that she'd refused to snuggle against him that night. His stubborn action had hurt her, again. He didn't like hurting her in any way. Still, he prayed he hadn't gotten her with child.

***

Rowan sat in one of the few chairs in front of the monstrous fireplace that filled nearly one whole wall of the great hall. When he'd led Gloriana into the keep's gathering place, he'd been glad to find a roaring fire. He was cold to the bone. She had been shivering so loudly her teeth chattered. He'd worried about her during this ride, but he'd worried even more as they'd ridden in the morning's foul weather. He'd known Thomas had been concerned as well. Yet there'd been naught to do but ride on and as fast as possible. She hadn't uttered one word of complaint. In truth, the few words he'd heard her speak this morn had been of her concern for the men. She had a good heart. She made a wife beyond compare, especially when she could put up with Thomas's moods…and with this odd relationship the three of them had fallen into.

He took a sip of ale from a mug one of the maids had brought him. While he'd sat here recovering from the morning's ride, Gloriana had flitted about the hall. She'd barely taken five minutes to warm in front of the fire before going off to "do her duties as the lord's wife," as she'd told him. Nearly every servant in the keep had managed to make their way into the hall to meet their new lady. She'd graciously smiled and accepted kind words of welcome, had returned hugs given her by children who had been drawn by the warmth of her personality. Even the near four dozen soldiers seated about the room as they kept out of the miserable day had been caught in her web of gentleness.

"What pleases you, Sir Rowan? Your eyes fairly dance with happiness." Gloriana walked over to the chair next to him carrying a mug of mead. She settled into the chair with a sigh.

"You, sweet Gloriana." He shook his head in amazement.

"Weariness shows in the circles under your eyes. Yet you have not sat down since we walked in here."

She blushed and pushed her long hair back over one shoulder. As soon as she'd shed her coat, she'd let free her wet braids so her hair could dry. He liked seeing it down. He wanted to run his hands through the silkiness of it. She was beautiful on the outside as well as the inside.

He watched her eyes drift closed for a few seconds. If he'd met her first, he might have changed his mind about not wanting to ever marry. He might have even given up making love with the occasional man to focus solely on pleasing this special woman. But he'd met Thomas before her. The hardened warrior had drawn him from the time in Tunis when Thomas had joined the battle beside him. They'd fought long and hard, both ending up wounded. There had been something about the power within Thomas's muscled body…something sad and lost in Thomas's intense blue eyes. Their coming together that first time had shocked them both, and been so damn hot. Nay, even as much as he was attracted to Gloriana, he could never give his lover up. Now he hoped to continue enjoying times with his *two* lovers. He longed to sink into her warmth, to drive deep within her. Yet he would not do so without

Thomas's approval. He could be nearly satisfied with only suckling at her breasts or feasting on her as he had already done.

Some sound amongst the noise around them jerked her awake. She blinked several times, yawned, and finally said, "Talk to me, Rowan. Keep me awake, for it is far too early to seek my bed."

*Bed.* Just the mention of the word had his body coming alive. He forced the reaction down. "About what, my lady?" He wasn't a man of idle chitchat, though he was definitely comfortable with her.

She looked intently at him. "Tell me about yourself, about the sadness I see so often in your eyes."

He stiffened and almost got up to walk away. He'd only shared pieces of his life with Thomas. As they'd sat around one campfire or another while they'd made their way back from the last Crusade battle, he'd bared his soul. Just as Thomas had bared his. Uneasy, he glanced around and found that they were well away from anyone else. Conversations and laughter were loud. Maids were flirting, and men were flirting right back. No one would hear them talking.

Because he'd taken too long to respond, she reached a small hand over to gently pat his knee and gain his attention. This time it wasn't his back that had stiffened. This time her tender touch brought his cock to full awareness. It throbbed and his pulse sped up. He knew his gaze was heated when he met hers and shook his head. "Twould be best if you don't touch me, Glori."

She blinked curiously and then seemed to understand his problem. Her gaze flicked down to where his shaft had begun pushing at the front of his braies and she quickly removed her hand. "I'm sorry." She blushed. "But, please, talk to me. Thomas is busy with the bailiff, tis too early for sup, too early to try to sleep."

Rowan drew in a breath and willed his erection to calm once more. He concentrated on the fire and slowly said, "We—you, Thomas, and me—are quite a threesome." He grimaced at the word choice. "I am not referring to our… well, to our lovemaking."

To his surprise, she gave a soft laugh and said quietly, "Twas very nice, this 'threesome' thing."

He felt his face heat and looked around once more to be sure they were still alone. When he saw that they were, his shoulders relaxed. "I meant that each of us has had a difficult time in life. Thomas, for example. He was raised to act the warrior from a young age. He has known almost nothing about a home and a family." Turning toward her, he saw that she listened avidly, eager to learn about her husband. "His mother died not long after his sister, Elizabeth, was born. A few years, I think. His father had no patience for children." He gripped his mug tightly once more. He and Thomas had both had brutish men for fathers. After a few seconds, he continued. "Although his daughter found a way past their father's defenses. Still, Thomas's father had little use for his son, fostering him out when he was but seven."

"So young," Gloriana whispered, her eyes misting.

"It made a man of him before he was truly old enough to go to war." Rowan couldn't tell her of the memories Thomas had shared with him of killing his first man when he was but six and ten. He couldn't tell her about the many other men he'd killed before becoming a knight at nine and ten. Deaths that still haunted Thomas many nights. "He has known only warring for most of his life."

She was quiet a minute, absorbing what he'd told her. Then she worried her lower lip before asking, "What of his first wife? Sarah? He said it was an arranged marriage." She fidgeted with the mug in her hands. "He said he didn't love her, or she him."

Rowan knew Thomas had already told her some about that earlier marriage. He'd probably told her some of his reasons why he didn't want to get her with child, but he decided to explain a bit more. "Thomas was betrothed to her at birth, as is common in some families. She was actually slightly older than him. And, no, there was no love between them." He took a second before continuing. "Thomas has felt guilty all these years since her death. He believes he should have stopped going off to battle when he learned of her being with child. She did not wish it."

Gloriana took another sip of mead, looking thoughtful. Rowan was almost certain that if she had been Thomas's first wife and was pregnant, Thomas would have stayed with her. He would not have wanted to be away from her during a time that could be difficult for a woman. With Sarah, he hadn't felt so possessive. He had let her convince him that he was needed more elsewhere. A decision he regretted to this day. He believed he'd failed her. "He claims they even argued about the matter. In the end he felt it best if he left for a while." He saw the concern for Thomas deepen in her expressive eyes. He wondered what else to tell her; what not to tell her. Rowan didn't tell her that Thomas believed Sarah might have had a lover, but not until after he'd gotten her pregnant.

Rowan thought maybe she'd hoped Thomas would die off in some battle so she could marry this other man. Rowan's anger at this unfaithful wife had him locking gazes with Gloriana. He ground out, "Thomas could have done nothing to keep her from dying giving birth to James."

Gloriana's eyes widened at the bitterness in his tone. "I'm sure tis true," she said, sitting back in her chair, looking uneasy at his flash of temper. He regretted having spoken so harshly. He sucked in a breath to calm down and gave her a weak smile. "I'm sorry, Glori. My feelings run strong toward Thomas, in defense of him."

She reached over to pat his hand. "I understand."

He relaxed even more at her gentle forgiving. "Thomas knows he couldn't have prevented her death. The knowledge of that is one thing, accepting it another." He hesitated and left the subject of Sarah. "Thomas loves his son, though he has never known how to show him."

Rowan looked away for a second, feeling the frustration of listening to Thomas many times as he discussed the matter. He didn't know how to help his friend, but he knew it was long past time that Thomas dealt with James.

"Each time they have seen each other over the years, Thomas hasn't been able to get past his formidable wish to control all things. Telling James that he is his father and that is all that matters has not been the best way to reach his son." Rowan glanced at Gloriana and caught her studying him.

"Thomas is good at being 'formidable.'" She gave a smile that hinted at warmth, even love. "He is a great leader of men, respected, as I've seen. But demanding, expecting, respect of a young boy… He needs help with James. And *I* will give it."

Rowan was struck by the determination that sparked in her eyes, the vehemence in her voice. Thomas was a very lucky man. "As will I, Glori. I will give whatever help I can."

"You are a good and loyal friend." Now her smile warmed for him and it touched him deeply. "Now you. I wish to know more about *you*."

Again, he looked at the fire and weighed in his mind just what to share with her. He decided a quick, blunt summary would be best. He gripped the mug in his hand tighter, and his stomach knotted from years of resentment. "I am the bastard son of the Duke of Remington. His oldest son. He acknowledged me at birth, but refused to marry my mother. He refused to have us even live with him."

He heard her small gasp, knew she'd have tears in her eyes for him. Her heart was far too soft. He couldn't bear to look at her right now.

"My mother, a tavern wench, and I lived above the tavern until she died of a fever when I was five." He ground his teeth and fought back the terrible loss he'd felt then, the horrid loneliness, the helplessness. "The Duke had married the daughter of another English duke by then. When the tavern owner took me to the Duke's home the night she died, he barely even looked at me. His wife wouldn't allow me in their home.

She couldn't stand the sight of me. So I left." "You left? But you were only five?" She sounded horrified.

Rowan hazarded a glance at Gloriana before looking away once more. Her eyes had smoldered with fury at this heartless duke, on Rowan's behalf. He couldn't remember anyone –other than Thomas—ever showing such passion toward anything that had happened to him. It took a couple of seconds for him to absorb the feeling of being cared for, of having someone being unconditionally on his side.

His voice was huskier than he would have liked when he continued with his story. "I found a group of minstrels leaving the village that night. They took me with them. Soon after, I began traveling with one group of soldiers or another."

He vowed that she would never learn of the horrors he'd survived. Even now, he fought to keep the images from finding a way into his mind. Too many hurts. Too many abuses. Until he'd become bigger, more muscled, harder than most of the other men. He'd grown skilled with a knife, better with a sword. By the time Edward had first called him to battle for the crown, few men would even consider challenging him. He was loyal to whomever he fought for, but he had never desired to stay with one lord and sign a knight's allegiance to him. *Until Thomas.*

"What you suffered… what you must have gone through…" He heard the catch in her voice. Again, it touched him more than he'd thought possible.

He blew out a ragged breath. "Tis all in the past, sweet Glori. I do not dwell on it. The Duke…"

He faced her and when she flinched, he wished he'd been able to control his expression better. "Is dead to me."

"But—"

Fortunately, at that moment Thomas walked toward them. He must have seen Rowan's angry expression too, for he asked with caution, "Are you all right?" He glanced at Gloriana in chastisement. "Has my wife said something to upset you?" Gloriana looked at him in annoyance. But Rowan spoke first, shaking his head in disgust at himself. "Nay. She has been kindly trying to learn more about me. Twas not her fault the subject was a foul one."

Thomas nodded in understanding and sympathy shone in his eyes. "Did you tell Glori that I offered you to hold Montrose for me? That Edward offered you your choice of several other holdings?"

Rowan frowned. The change of subject from his past was good, but he didn't like talking about having a castle of his own.

"Nay! You are *not* considering any of that, are you?" Gloriana looked fierce as she faced him. And then glared at Thomas. "Do you *really* want that? Want our Rowan to live somewhere else? I thought you said…"

Now Thomas looked angry. "I have never wanted him anywhere but with me. But Rowan has earned the right to a holding of his own."

She sat back in her chair, but her eyes no longer flashed in outrage. "I misspoke. I am sorry."

Talking about his troubled past had been painful. But seeing and hearing the strength of what Gloriana and Thomas felt about him soothed his soul once more. She'd said "*our Rowan.*" This was the closest to a family as he'd ever had. He could not give them up! Not unless it would someday be necessary. And then it would probably kill him.

Rowan swallowed down the lump in his throat. "Do not fret, Gloriana, I have no desire to live anywhere but at Middlemound." He met and held Thomas's gaze. "All I desire is at Middlemound."

***

Two mornings later, Gloriana dressed quietly and prepared to leave her still sleeping husband to go down to break her fast. She hesitated at the door and glanced back at him lying there naked and stretched so temptingly across their rumpled bed. Her heart raced; her woman's place grew moist, hot. But he was worn out this morn. He'd been so passionate the night before, shown her more wondrous acts of lovemaking. He'd feasted on her and, oh my heavens, she really was beginning to like that greatly.

She quietly closed the door and started down the hallway, still thinking about the complex man who was her husband. Respected by so many and with good reason. An anxious father uncertain how to deal with his son. Loved by both Rowan and her. And an amazing lover to her alone, one who drew out her long-buried passionate nature more each time he bedded her.

Her cheeks heated at how daring she'd been late last night. She'd feasted on him as well. Watching Rowan take Thomas's cock into his mouth had intrigued her. She'd wanted to try it herself ever since then. At first wary that she could take his great rod into her small mouth, Thomas had finally allowed her to try it. She smiled at how awkward she'd felt. It had taken great effort to accommodate him, but she'd done it. Hearing his groan of enjoyment, seeing the strained look of pleasure on his face… She would savor those memories and looked forward to the experience again.

She continued down the stairs and to the great hall. She visited with a few of the early rising soldiers and a couple of the maids who brought her bread and mead. But she was anxious to get back to Thomas. Her woman's place was still quivering with anticipation. Mayhap he would be roused by now, ready to…

*Stop thinking about it! Thomas has more than just meeting your needs to worry about.* Still, she had a difficult time thinking about anything else as she climbed the stairs with a chunk of bread and a mug of mead for Thomas. Her foolish mind circled back to how Thomas had then taken her in the way he took Rowan.

Her stomach fluttered at the memory. He'd put her on all fours, which she'd found uncomfortable at first. But he'd lightly stroked her back, caressed her bare buttocks, and gentled her like a nervous mare. She'd been trembling by then and ready for more. Thomas had taken great care to prepare her small hole, much more cautiously than he'd done with Rowan. But then Rowan was experienced at it.

She stilled, remembering how Thomas had held her hips, how he'd slowly inserted his thick shaft into her tender bottom. She'd gasped and frozen in place, uncertain she could actually take him inside her body in that way. He'd mumbled soothing words to her. He'd been careful with each move forward. But finally he'd driven all of his length into her.

She shuddered, almost feeling the fullness once again. She drew in a calming breath. No wonder Rowan's face scrunched up the way it did when Thomas thrust into him from behind!

Gloriana was so lost in her thoughts that she had missed seeing Rowan coming toward her from the hallway. He stopped just in front of her at the top of the stairs, catching her arm to steady her when she flinched in surprise.

He looked worriedly down at her. "Are you all right?" Gloriana's face flamed and she couldn't meet his eyes. Her loose tongue spoke before she could control what she said. "I know how you feel… when…"

"When what?"

She stepped onto the landing, and then glanced backward. "When… you know what I mean."

Rowan's brow was furrowed in confusion. She wished she'd never said anything, but now she was determined to finish this. She leaned closer and said in a loud whisper, "Thomas put his… his rod… in my…" She glanced behind her again and then back at his widened eyes. "In my other place. Like he does you."

"God's teeth, Gloriana!" Thomas hissed having suddenly walked up behind Rowan. "Tis a private matter!"

Rowan was gaping at her, and then he began laughing.

Thomas scowled.

Gloriana huffed and tossed the bread at her husband, which made Rowan laugh harder.

After a second, he managed to ask, "And did you like it, my sweet Glori? As much as I do?" His eyes sparked with amusement as he looked at Thomas.

She ignored her husband's heavy sigh of irritation.

"In truth, I found it rather odd at first. Not being covered from behind. No, that was pleasant enough. But having his…" She glanced at Thomas, who was now looking stunned at her boldness. "Having his mighty shaft… pushed into me there. It took some getting used to."

"Aye, it does."

Rowan chuckled and walked by them and down the stairs. "I'll get the men up and about, prepare to leave. While you deal with your saucy wife." Thomas waited a second and then frowned at her. "Mayhap you should stay here, wife. You are becoming bolder with each day. I am almost afraid what you will say in front of Elizabeth and Abernon."

"What I will say, husband, is that James is coming home with us to Middlemound. Or else my fierce husband will bring battle to their castle. And I will be right at his side."

## Chapter Eight

Thomas coughed, harder than he'd been doing all morn. It shook his whole body, made his horse dance nervously beneath him. He didn't have time for being ill, nor did he want to draw attention to his growing weakness. He covered the next cough with his fisted hand, annoyed. It was mid-morn of the third day since they'd left Montrose. The weather had continued to be colder than normal, off-and-on rainy, and the wind blustery at times. They were all more than ready to get to Castle Abernon. And so it was a relief when Thomas at last spotted the dark gray stone of the castle's walls. He raised a hand to halt his party well back from the fortress. His men needed rest, the warmth of a fire-heated great hall, and food. Gloriana hadn't said a word all morn, but he knew she could barely sit a saddle now. He could barely sit one himself. Every time he looked at his small wife and saw the darkening circles of exhaustion around her eyes and the way her shoulders slumped in weariness, he felt guilt for putting her through this. He would have left her behind at Middlemound had not

Abernon insisted she and Rowan accompany him here. He would have gone against even that demand and left her at Montrose, but she'd refused to consider it. She fully intended on being at this meeting.

*Meeting.* More like an argument—heated, probably—about whether or not the almighty Lord Abernon would let Thomas have *his* own son.

He gripped the reins tightly. Beneath him his destrier shifted uneasily, as if he sensed his rider's anger. Thomas desperately wanted to get this confrontation over with, yet he was reluctant to send one of his men forward to request permission to enter the castle's grounds. As he sat staring at the formidable castle, he once again thought about his son. He hadn't seen James in nearly two years. In truth, he had barely seen him during the boy's ten years of life. *What kind of a father was he?*

*Father. Graham Lancaster,* his *father. Damn the man's soul.*

Darkness and anger filled Thomas at the thought of his hardened warlord father. A man who had only gotten his wife with child, twice, because she'd begged him to do so. He'd spent as little time as possible with Thomas, sending him away to foster out at seven, far younger than was common. Yet the man had a weakness, at times, for Elizabeth. Thomas had always been glad for that. But he'd never been able to forgive his father for casting him aside. Even after all these years the pain of rejection ran deep. *Is that what his son felt?* Elizabeth had told Thomas that she'd always tried to make James feel loved, even telling him that his father loved him enough to let him live with Gavin and her.

He looked toward the formidable castle where his beloved sister lived. He was truly grateful to her—even to Abernon—for giving his son a good home all these years. But he knew it wasn't the same as having your blood father with you. Not that he knew what that was like, either. Even though he'd been Graham's heir, he'd turned down the holding to let his sister have it for her dowry. He'd gone on battling, because that was all he'd really known how to do. When he'd gained Montrose and a wife he hadn't wanted, he, too, had had a child that he didn't know what to do with. The difference between his father and him was that he'd loved his son. He hadn't cast James aside, at least not in his opinion. He'd given him a better life than he could have provided. Then. But things had changed. And, God in heaven, he regretted all the years of separation from James.

His thoughts returned to Gloriana, waiting somewhere quietly behind him. He had been blessed with a gentle wife this time, one who would make a great mother. With her help, he hoped to become a decent father… if it wasn't too late. The main problem with his wife was that she was eight years younger than he and she wanted a babe of her own. He knew she would act the mother to James, but she longed for a child he could give her. He'd been against that, fearing she would die as Sarah had giving birth. As she'd told him, he knew that most women did not die that way. During the ride here, he'd begun wondering if his true fear was in failing again as a father, as he'd done so far with James.

He coughed, shivered beneath his fur-lined cloak. His body was growing sore from coughing so much this morn. His ribs ached, as did all of him from his neck down. And he'd started feeling lightheaded about an hour ago. He'd tried not to let anyone see how poorly he was feeling. He'd kept to himself as much as possible. Nothing would keep him from this meeting!

The sound of hoofbeats growing closer had him straightening in his saddle. *Rowan and Gloriana.* They'd no doubt grown impatient with his long silence and unexplained need to stop. He fought down the urge to cough again as they approached.

"Is there a problem, my lord?" Rowan asked loud enough for the men waiting behind them to hear. "Or shall I send a messenger forward?"

Thomas heard the concern in his friend's tone. "Nay, there is nay problem. I only needed a moment of thought." Although he tried not to, he did cough now, lifting a hand to cover his mouth. "Tis time we sought hospitality from Abernon. The men need rest and food."

As Gloriana rode up beside him, he added, "My wife needs rest and food, too." Another chill swept over him.

Her brow furrowed. "As do you, husband." She studied him intently.

Thomas felt hot and when he turned from glancing at his wife, he swayed a bit in his saddle. He caught himself and stiffened, hoping Gloriana hadn't noticed.

But she had. "Thomas? What is wrong?"

He didn't want to talk about it and shook his head, which only made him more lightheaded. "Tis nothing more than weariness. As we all suffer from."

Rowan's frown told him he believed his actions were from more than being tired. Yet he didn't comment and turned to ride back to find a man to send with the announcement of their arrival.

Gloriana didn't look satisfied with his excuse, but she gave a nod of acceptance…for now. He knew she would question him later. Her gaze turned to the dark, sprawling castle ahead. "Not a very welcoming sight, is it?"

"Abernon is an ancient castle, built as an imposing, formidable fortress." He coughed again, pain swelling in his chest.

Gloriana edged her horse closer and reached over to touch his thigh. "Thomas, tell me what is wrong? The color has left your face, yet there is a red sheen beneath your beard. Your eyes, they look glazed."

His shoulders shuddered, yet he felt beads of sweat on his forehead. "Do not worry. It is exhaustion, no more than that."

Before she could offer a protest, they heard the loud workings of the wooden wheels and metal gears turning in the distance. He looked toward the castle and saw the drawbridge being lowered, and then the portcullis rising. A guard on the parapet above the gatehouse waved a flag, letting them know they were being allowed to enter.

Thomas didn't have to look back to know that each of his men had tensed. All knew why their lord had forced them to travel through miserable weather at a tiring speed. They wanted this confrontation over nearly as much as he did. And he knew if he chose to fight for his son—even against unfavorable odds—they would do so. He'd chosen his most loyal, most battle-strong soldiers to accompany him. Still, now he was even more reluctant to take Gloriana into Abernon's castle. He wanted her safe, not part of any sort of battle. He could leave her here with one or two of his best men.

As if she sensed his thoughts, she snapped, "Do not even think of leaving me behind! I go where you go, my lord." Rowan returned to ride at his side, his expression hard. "As do I," he said in a tone that would allow no discussion. He raised a hand and motioned the men forward.

Resigned, Thomas urged his mount to take the lead once more.

***

Gloriana refused to lag behind while her husband prepared to face this difficult situation. Although he scowled sideways at her, she insisted on riding alongside him. "Tis my rightful place," she stated, as they guided their horses across the long wooden bridge passing over the castle's wide moat. She wrinkled her nose at the stench of foul water.

Thomas didn't respond, but she knew his irritation. And when their party was met by several dozen well-armed soldiers in the bailey, she felt irritation herself. *Nay, more than that! Anger.*

"How dare Lord Abernon present a show of force as we enter his grounds! This is your sister's home, too." She bristled in outrage beneath her warm cloak.

"Watch your words, Gloriana," Thomas bit out, giving her a sharp look before focusing ahead once more. He walked his horse a few feet forward and left her behind.

Her hackles rose even more, but she held her tongue and followed his gaze. A man mayhap five or ten years older than Thomas and every bit as powerfully built stood in full chainmail at the foot of the keep's steps. The expression on his leanly handsome face was not of welcome. His narrowed eyes looked in challenge at Thomas, and then at Rowan, who had ridden up beside her.

"Lord Middlemound," the man said, sounding bitter. "Sir Rowan, I assume." His tone remained hostile. He didn't even bother acknowledging her. Before her husband could react or respond, a stunning woman with flowing, long black hair much like Thomas's rushed out of the keep. She held up her long skirt and scurried down the steps to stop in front of Abernon. Gloriana couldn't see the look she gave him, but assumed it was one of chastisement for he frowned, yet didn't say anything more.

In the next moment, she hurried closer. A wide smile of delight filling her face. "Thomas. Oh, Thomas. I'm so very glad to see you."

He started to speak, coughed instead. He swayed a bit in the saddle.

"Thomas?" Elizabeth questioned, looking worried.

Gloriana immediately urged her mount closer to him.

He coughed again, harder. His face pinched as he closed his eyes and swayed even more.

"Thomas!" she cried.

"I...I..." His head lolled and he shifted precariously on his horse. Gloriana all but leapt to the muddy ground, stumbling for a second, caught in the yards of her skirt. She rushed to him just as he slid from the saddle. They went to the ground together. She landed flat on her back; he landed on top of her, nearly crushing her.

"Husband!" she gasped under his great weight. Her heart thundered in panic. She glanced toward the only man nearby that she trusted. "Rowan! Rowan, come help me." Suddenly there was confusion all around her.

Thomas's men were scrambling to dismount and attempting to surround and guard their fallen lord. Abernon's men drew closer, alarmed by the other armed men's clear tension. A bad situation was quickly becoming much worse, and she feared what might happen. But she worried far more over her beloved than the disgruntled men nearby.

"Thomas." She gently patted his face to awaken him. "Thomas, please wake up."

Rowan hurried to her side, kneeling beside her. His strained expression showed the same worry she felt as Thomas remained silent and unmoving. "Are you all right?" he asked.

She could barely breathe, but her discomfort mattered not.

"He...he won't awaken." She felt tears stinging her eyes. "Why won't he awaken?" "Thomas will be all right," Rowan assured her, though the tension in his face revealed his concern. "We both know he is a strong man."

She struggled beneath her husband. "He is a heavy man as well." Yet even though he continued to squash her, Gloriana was reluctant to let him go.

Rowan was about to reach for Thomas when Elizabeth shoved her way through the many soldiers to kneel in the mud next to Rowan. He stiffened and sat back, but Gloriana held his gaze and silently told him to stay with her. She didn't know any of these people, didn't trust any of them. Only Rowan and Thomas's men.

He gave a slight nod.

"What happened? What is wrong with him?" Elizabeth asked in obvious distress. She gently touched Thomas's leg. "Oh, Thomas."

Abernon moved to stand above his wife, his expression unreadable but still unfriendly. "He should not have come here if he is ill."

Gloriana watched fury spread over Rowan's face, saw anger fill the faces of Thomas's men. If she weren't buried beneath her great lummox of a husband, she would... Well, she wasn't sure what she would do, but it would be bad.

Since she couldn't do anything else, she glared up at Abernon.

"My husband is ill because of you! We have been forced to ride through God-awful weather to come here at your command." Tears trickled down her cheeks as she ran a trembling hand overThomas's face. Alarm spread through her. "Now he's hot with fever. Ill enough to pass out."

"You cannot speak to me in such a disrespectful manner," Abernon said, in a warning growl.

Thomas's men looked threatening. Rowan prepared to stand, reaching for the knife in his boot.

Abernon's men put hands to their weapons.

But Gloriana ignored all of them but Abernon. "When you have earned my respect, I shall give it. You have not. All I know for now is that this—my husband being ill—is *your* fault!"

His chest puffed up in outrage.

Elizabeth stood, turning to glower at her husband. "Enough! My brother is clearly ill; nothing else matters."

He had the grace—or good sense, in her opinion —to back down. Although Gloriana had stepped on his pride, he grumbled an apology she couldn't quite hear. Then he heaved a resigned sigh and said, "Get him inside the keep and to a bedchamber."

Elizabeth gifted her husband with an appreciative look, which appeared to calm him even more. Then she turned to Rowan. "Can you and one of your men carry my brother?"

Abernon stepped close again. "I can help."

"Nay, you will not touch him." She pinned him with a look that had him grinding his jaw once more. "Until he is well enough to deal with you, I would rather you keep your distance from him."

Gloriana decided right then that she liked Thomas's sister.

But before anymore could be said or done, Thomas moaned and drew everyone's attention. He raised his head, blinked away obvious fogginess, and said in shock, "God's teeth! What happened?"

He awkwardly shifted until he could glance in embarrassment at Gloriana. "Wife?" His eyes still looked a bit unfocused. "Are you all right?"

The tension broke around them, replaced by relief and concern. "Aye, but I would be better without your great weight crushing me into the mud." She tried to give him a weak smile, tried not to let him see her tears of happiness.

He attempted to struggle to his feet, finally being helped by Rowan. Then, still looking unsteady, Thomas reached to pull her upright. "I am sorry," he said, coughing, wincing from the effort of it.

Gloriana's coat was sodden with mud, as was her hair and boots. Yet none of her discomfort mattered when her husband was clearly ill. "We must get you inside, my lord. Into a bed. You need rest and some of my medicinals."

Her stubborn husband was back in a flash, which amused her a bit. He thrust his shoulders back and his hard jaw up. He scowled from her to his sister. "This is foolishness. I am fine. Tis but a cough, no more."

Elizabeth rolled her eyes and looked past him to Gloriana. "Why is it men can be so impossible at times? Especially when they are obviously not well." She shook her head at Thomas. "The bigger, the tougher… the more foolish."

"Elizabeth," Abernon protested, only to be frowned into silence.

She focused on Rowan again. "See to it that your lord, my contrary brother, gets into the keep. I will have the maids bring a bathing tub and water up the bedchamber I have already prepared for Thomas and his wife."

Then she looked to Gloriana. "I am Elizabeth, by the way. I am sorry to have met you in this unfortunate manner."

Gloriana grimaced at the sad state of her appearance before her new sister-in-law. "Gloriana. And, aye, I would rather have been more presentable."

When she saw her husband beginning to sway once more, she hurried forward to put herself under one of his arms. Rowan took his other arm to help shoulder the unsteady weight of their lord. "Let us seek out that chamber and put my husband to bed."

Thomas grumbled under his breath, but didn't put up any resistance as they led him from the bailey.

***

Nearly a day passed as Gloriana stayed by the bed to care for her sick husband. She'd given him every medicinal she could think of to help with his deep, ragged cough. She'd wiped his heated face and fevered chest with cool water. Her arms ached from her efforts, as did her body. She needed to sleep, but she would not until he was truly on his way back from whatever ailment had set upon him. She hated seeing him brought low like this; he disliked it even more, though he'd had few rational moments since being put to bed.

Unable to sit a moment longer on the hard chair near the bed, she stood and stretched. His fever had finally broken but an hour ago and he slept more restfully. The worst was over; she was sure of it.

She turned to look first at Elizabeth, standing on the other side of the bed, and then at Rowan, hovering by the windows. Neither had left for more than a few minutes in all this time. "I think you can both leave now, seek rest yourselves."

"You need rest as well, my lady," Rowan said in concern. "I will sit with him while you go to my chamber and …"

Gloriana shook her head, making him smile in understanding. "Nay, I will stay here until Thomas fully awakens." She looked to Elizabeth.

The gentle-yet-fierce woman had been quiet much of the time she'd helped wash her brother down. She'd spent much time tenderly holding one of his hands; her love for Thomas was obvious. She'd also spent much time quietly studying both Gloriana and Rowan.

Elizabeth had been worried about Thomas and had seemed to respect the depths of worry they had as well. Gloriana had felt uncomfortable knowing she was being judged in some way, Rowan, too. But she'd decided to give her sister-in-law time to make her judgments and prayed she would make the right ones. She tensed now that Elizabeth looked seriously toward them.

"My brother has suffered much in life. I had no idea how much until now." She gently tucked the linen higher over his chest. "It is good he has people who care about him." She glanced toward Rowan. "Someone who understands what he has gone through."

Gloriana remained silent, waiting for Rowan to respond. She knew what Elizabeth referred to. She, too, had listened to the fevered ramblings and anguished cries of her husband through the long hours of the night. Her heart had ached watching him toss about, hearing him experience again one battle after another. He'd cried out his sorrow at having killed one man, and then another. Each death claimed a part of his soul.

After a few seconds, Rowan said cautiously, "Aye, I care for him, and I understand what he suffers."

He faced the window, leaned his arms beside it and sighed heavily. "Tis never easy to take someone's life, even in wars where you have no choice. Good men, like Thomas, never forget."

"Aye, Thomas is a good man, no thanks to our father," Elizabeth stated quietly, sounding bitter. "You have fought long beside my brother?"

"Nay, we have only known each other since the battles in Tunis. He saved my life." Gloriana heard the strain in Rowan's voice and remembered some of what Thomas had told her. "You saved his life as well."

Elizabeth seemed to weigh what they'd said before speaking again. "And you are prepared to fight by his side again, are you not, Sir Rowan?" Elizabeth asked with uneasiness in her tone. "If it would come to fighting my husband for Thomas's son, you would be at my brother's side?"

He faced her with steely determination on his face. "I will *always* fight at Thomas's side. My loyalty to him is unconditional."

"As is mine," Gloriana inserted. "Although I would hope it not necessary, I will hold a sword in battle right alongside both Thomas and Rowan."

Once more Elizabeth studied them in silence for a couple of minutes. Then she gave a weak smile. "My brother is blessed to have two such devoted people who care so much for him."

She held Rowan's gaze. "Who love him."

Rowan tensed and Gloriana understood his concern. She would not have him upset, not have him shunned because of his love for her husband. She straightened to her full height and faced her sister-in-law. "There is nothing wrong with the way Rowan and my husband feel about one another. Nothing."

"Nay, not in my opinion, either. But I had wondered how you truly felt, Sir Rowan. Now I know." Elizabeth hesitated. "It bothers me not what happens between you and Thomas. Although I admit to being a bit confused with Gloriana now his wife." Gloriana wasn't sure what to say and Rowan appeared to be as tongue-tied as her. The subject was a delicate one.

"None of this has to do with me. I only want to see Thomas happy. James, too." She heaved a sigh. "It is my husband who is the problem. He is quite opposed to men who…" she blushed, "to men who love other men. Yet you, Sir Rowan, greatly puzzle him."

"Puzzle him? Why is that?" Gloriana couldn't help asking, glancing from Rowan and back to Elizabeth.

Elizabeth looked at Rowan, in admiration and in curiosity. "Sir Rowan's reputation with women is well-known. He is something of a legend really. Still, it is known that he has relations from time to time with men." Gloriana knew of Rowan's reputation with women. Marie had praised him in a private moment of gossip. And, after her own limited experience with only one of his talents, she understood it. She'd also known he'd been with other men before Thomas, but she hadn't been aware that part of his life was talked about. She'd not seen any of the Middlemound men or Montrose men showing any dislike for being around him. Probably because they were jealous of his reputation with women.

"How do you know of my relations with Thomas?" Rowan asked darkly, interrupting Gloriana's musings.

Elizabeth shifted uneasily and looked at her brother. It took her a moment before she answered. "One of our former knights was a man you had… well, bedded."

Rowan tensed, his face drawing tight. Gloriana worried about him and was feeling uncertain about Elizabeth. She would support Rowan however she could.

"Before you tossed him aside for Thomas in Tunis," Elizabeth continued, again looking curiously at Rowan. "Or so the man claimed." Her expression softened as she glanced from Rowan to Thomas and back to Rowan. "Clearly, he had been unhappy to lose your…your attentions."

Gloriana watched Elizabeth as she swept her gaze over Rowan's powerful, handsome body. She saw the flare of interest in her eyes. Gloriana felt a second of jealousy before letting it go. But it irritated her that someone had deliberately tried to cause a problem for Thomas and Rowan.

"Rowan is not a callous lover. He is very loyal." Both Elizabeth and Rowan glanced at Gloriana's fierce defense of him. True, she hadn't known him long, but she had decided to love him along with Thomas. She didn't love easily, but when she did love, her loyalty was steadfast. "And I do not like someone going about spreading tales about Thomas, either."

Elizabeth smiled in approval. "Nor would I, but the man is dead now. His tales died with him. As far as I know, he only told my husband about the matter one time when they were sharing drinks together. He tried to spark an interest in Abernon, which didn't end well for him."

She heaved a deep sigh. "But his admission angered my husband. It made Gavin even more determined to keep James from Thomas."

Rowan fisted his hands at his sides. "He cannot judge Thomas by this matter! And, know you this; I am your brother's first and only male lover." He ground his jaw. "Know you this as well, I will walk away from him forever if necessary. Thomas needs and deserves his son."

Gloriana gasped at his warning. "Nay, Rowan!"

Thomas stirred on the bed and drew their attention. His eyes were slightly glazed with weakness, but he said grimly, "You will not walk away from me." He drew in a ragged breath, struggling not to cough. "I want my son, but I will not make such a great sacrifice as to lose you."

"Thomas," Rowan began.

But Thomas shook his head to stop his protest. "My son does not even want to be with me. He hates me. He told me as much the last time I tried to speak with him about coming to Montrose with me."

Gloriana, and clearly Rowan too, hadn't known about that. She gaped at him. *How could James have spoken so cruelly to his father? How could he have hurt him so badly?* Were he here in front of her, she would have shaken him by his ears.

It was Elizabeth who said softly, "James was but eight when he said that. He had not seen you since two years before that time. He hardly knows you, Thomas. You cannot hold a child's fears against him."

At once Gloriana regretted her angered thoughts about the boy.

"She is right, husband," Gloriana said. "I feared you, too, when I first met you. You can be rather intimidating. I can only imagine what a mere lad would think of you, a father to him and yet a stranger."

"You no longer fear me, wife." Thomas's gaze softened as he accepted her gentleness, her reasoning. "Mayhap there is hope that I can become less fearful to James as well." He looked to his sister. "I wish to see James on the morrow, when I am stronger and out of this bed."

Elizabeth worried her lower lip before saying, "He is not here, brother. Gavin fostered him to our neighbor over a month ago." Thomas sat up, had to brace himself on his arms, and glowered murderously. "Yet he said *nothing* of this in the message he sent to me? Yet he demanded—aye, demanded—that I come here with my wife and Rowan to talk to him about James?"

She shook her head, looking guilty. "Nay, he refused to even answer your message. It was *I* who wanted you all to come here. *I* who hope to find a way for you and my husband to make peace. *I* who want you to make peace with your son. But first it must be made with Gavin. He can be a very trying, very stubborn man."

Gloriana had been listening in amazement, surprised at Elizabeth's manipulation and daring, impressed as well. "Yet your husband allowed us entry here. Even when he clearly either strongly dislikes Thomas or hates him."

Now Elizabeth smiled in mischief. "A wife has her ways. He likes sharing a bed with me more than sleeping alone."

Gloriana blinked and then giggled. "We really must get to know one another better." Rowan snorted, though he sounded amused.

Thomas lay back and grumbled about conniving women. Then he reached for Gloriana's arm and tugged her so that she all but fell on the bed beside him. "I will confront Abernon on the morrow. For now I need to have my lady at my side, making me feel better, showing me her wifely ways."

Elizabeth walked toward the door, nodded for Rowan to follow her. "There is a maid here who says she knows you. She has asked to see you again, if you were interested." Rowan glanced back at Thomas and Gloriana. His gaze heated, but he sighed and left the chamber. "As long as I do not have to face your husband…" His words trailed off as he closed the door, but Gloriana worried for him.

***

Thomas had been watching Gloriana sleep for about an hour, worried at the dark circles of weariness still under her eyes. Their ride here had taken much out of her. And then she'd nursed him through his illness. But the tempting scent of her, the ache of longing he felt were too powerful now. He gently shifted her hair out of his way and nibbled at her neck.

She stirred, slowly coming awake. He trailed the tip of his tongue over her small ear lobe and she shivered. "Wife, I have need of you," he said huskily.

He shifted over her, careful to not crush her, and rubbed his hard cock against her woman's place.

She smiled up at him and spread her legs. "Tis fortunate then that I have need of you, husband."

He put a hand over her mound, slid a finger inside and grinned, pleased to find her moist already. "You are ready for me."

"Always." She put a hand to his face and studied him for a second. "You are sure you are up to this?"

Thomas used his arms to brace himself above her and drove inside in one long slide. He sighed in satisfaction. "Most definitely."

With a sigh of her own, she clasped her legs around his back. "I have missed this, my lord. I am most impatient." She arched up to meet his drives.

"As am I." Well pleased with his wife, Thomas gave way to his fierce need of her. He took her steadily faster and faster. Thrust deeper and deeper, grunting as she worked him with her clenching inner muscles.

All too soon he felt her explode around him, heard her precious cries of release. He, too, reached that point but tried to force her legs to free him, panting in strain when she refused to let go.

"Glori, you must—"

She glowered up at him and held him tighter. "Nay! You will *not* pull out of me this time." "You have not drunk the tea," he gritted out, grimacing in near-pain as he fought against shooting into her body. "I must—"

"I drank your special tea only the one time, Thomas. I poured it out the window each time after that."

"You *what?*" he growled. She had betrayed him, gone against his wishes. He tried to withdraw again.

She refused to allow it, pushed her legs down on his back with more strength than he'd thought she had. This time he couldn't stop himself.

The desperate need in him was too strong. Her warmth around his throbbing cock was too much. His body went wild. He pumped in and out frantically until he roared out at the same time he filled her with his seed.

With a satisfied sigh, she lowered her legs.

But Thomas was furious. He rolled off of her and climbed out of the bed. "You deceived me."

"Did you not deceive me as well by forcing those teas upon me?" Her face was grim with anger, too.

"I had already told you I could not give you a child," he gritted out, pacing the room. She sat up in the bed, and he tried not to look at the naked woman he treasured, yet now felt betrayed by.

"What will you do if we find that I am, in fact, with child? Will you force a tonic down me to get rid of the babe?"

He heard the fear in her voice and saw the tears in her eyes. But it was his own fears that held him captive right now. Fear of losing her in birthing. Fear of failing another child as a father. He found his braies and pulled them on, and then his tunic and boots. He strode toward the door, stopping to look back at her.

"I could not do that, but I am not sure I can live with a wife who tried to trick me."

He opened the door, walked out and closed it, and then leaned back against it in turmoil. He listened in anguish to her heartbroken cry of, "Yet I was expected to let you trick me."

## Chapter Nine

*God, what have I done?* Thomas drew in a deep breath filled with shame at the way he'd treated Gloriana. He'd have to find a way to make things right between them. She was forcing him to truly face his feelings about having another child. As Rowan had told him many times, he was being a fool about the matter. She wasn't asking too much of him, but he'd been willing to give too little of himself.

He rubbed a hand through his hair, trying to calm down. What exactly were his reasons for not wanting to have another child? He'd long claimed—to himself—that he couldn't risk endangering another woman to give him another child. Sarah shouldn't have died because of giving birth to James. And yet she'd wanted a baby. She'd known the risks of childbirth and accepted them. The worst had happened in her case, but it wasn't anyone's fault…not his and not hers. It had simply happened. Losing Sarah had been a tragedy that he'd felt guilty about for many reasons. But losing Gloriana… He closed his eyes and struggled against the nearly overwhelming fear that filled him at such an idea. He couldn't imagine his life now without her in it. But she desperately wanted a baby, so much that she was willing to risk going behind his back by not drinking the tea he'd tried to force upon her. He still didn't think she'd known exactly what it was, but she'd evidently sensed something. They had tricked each other. And he hated that.

Thomas shoved away from the door. It was time he started dealing with the jumble he'd made of his life. He'd take back control one step at a time, beginning with confronting Gavin Campbell. With that goal in mind, he marched down the long hallway to the lord's bedchamber. Dawn was approaching and he fully intended to be on his way to get James within the hour.

Thomas pounded on the heavy wooden door, unconcerned if he infringed on a private moment between his sister and her husband.

"Abernon! I must talk to you. Now!" "After we break our fast," Gavin called back, sounding annoyed.

"Now!" Thomas would not be put off. "If I have to break down this door to talk to you, I will."

He heard the rustling of bed linens, followed by angry footsteps crossing the wood floor. Then softer footsteps hurried after the first ones.

It was Elizabeth who opened the door. She looked worriedly at him, standing there in her chemise with her fiercely scowling husband behind her. "Should you be out of bed? Are you all right?"

Thomas couldn't help softening a bit at her concern. "I am much better this morn. Do not fret about me." He still felt weaker than he should, but it wasn't going to stop him from what he intended to do.

With that in mind, he fixed his gaze on Gavin. The man of similar height and build was naked and appeared not to care about the fact. His wide shoulders were stiff, and he clearly didn't want Thomas there right now. But Thomas was determined to see this through.

"We talk in private, or we talk in here with Elizabeth present. It matters naught to me. But I *will* speak with you now. I *will* know to which of your neighbors you have sent *my* son."

Gavin's mouth tightened and his eyes flashed with warning. He looked ready to physically lift Elizabeth out of the way. Again, his sister intervened. She nudged her husband back and made room for Thomas to enter the room. "I will hear this discussion." She gave neither man a choice.

His brow wrinkled in vexation, and then Gavin stormed across the chamber to drag on his braies. He didn't bother with donning a tunic. At the same time he went to partially dress, Elizabeth went to retrieve a cloak from atop a second trunk and pulled it over her nightclothes.

Thomas closed the door behind him and tried to control his temper. He stood there, fisting his hands at his sides, torn between doing what he'd come here for or going back to Gloriana and begging her forgiveness. Evidently Elizabeth picked up on part of his distress, maybe because he kept glancing at the door.

"You have argued with your wife, have you not?" his sister questioned, disapproval and sympathy on her pretty face. "I recognize the guilt in your expression; see how you fight not to go back to her."

His gaze darted to Gavin, who actually appeared calmer now.

They shared a man's second of understanding about dealing with a woman. Once more Thomas pulled on his patience. "Tis a private matter, but one I must deal with later. She needs time away from me for now. Time to—"

Elizabeth sighed and shook her head. "Time to remember how much she loves you." Thomas closed his eyes for a second and blew out a frustrated breath. "I can only hope she loves me enough."

He focused on Gavin once more. "We have two issues to settle, Abernon. I cannot fix my problem with Gloriana until I deal with these issues."

Gavin perched on the edge of a trunk by one of the windows. A cool breeze fluttered the edges of the oiled paper window covering behind him. The candle on the bedside table flickered, and the smell of melting wax drifted about the chamber. As he stretched out his long legs, the man narrowed his eyes. "I assume you want to talk about Rowan and James."

"Listen to my brother, husband. Be as fair in your judgment with him as you are in dealing with your many people." Elizabeth stood beside him and put a gentle hand on his leg. "You are a good man, this I know."

He nodded, seemed to slump a bit at her manipulation. "Speak."

It irritated Thomas that he couldn't read his brother-in-law's expression. His jaw was set; his posture was stiff. Yet he appeared to be waiting and ready to listen. Thomas prayed he'd have the patience to not make matters worse. Much depended on what he said now.

He forced himself to meet Gavin's eyes. "Elizabeth has already explained to me that you have been told Rowan and I are lovers. I will not deny the truth of it."

His stomach knotted as he watched the other man's face, saw the expected tightening of the muscles in his cheeks. He really didn't want to have to explain himself, but he made an effort anyway. "What happened between us came about due to certain circumstances. Understand that I make no excuses for what we did. Nor for what we continue to do." He watched his brother-in-law. "Until Rowan, I was never drawn to another man, could not even imagine being so."

Gavin studied him intently, but remained silent. Elizabeth kept her calming hand on his leg, gently squeezed it.

Thomas thought about Rowan. He thought about the horrors his friend had survived growing up and yet turned into a man of such loyalty, such honor. "There is no other man that I trust with my life or with Gloriana. We went through much, fighting on the battlefields together in Tunis. We saved each other's lives time and again. Our bond was special because of that. The other ... cannot be explained. It just is. In truth, I care not how you feel about my relationship with Rowan."

"What about Gloriana?" Gavin asked.

This wasn't something Thomas wanted to talk about in front of his sister. He hesitated, trying to figure out what to say.

"Gloriana loves Rowan, too, husband," Elizabeth said softly. "As we cared for Thomas while he was ill, neither would leave his side for long. I observed them. I saw the way she looked at him and saw how she worried about him."

She looked from Gavin back to Thomas. "While her feelings are strong for your first knight, brother, it is *you* who owns her heart. There are many levels of love, from what I have observed. You are fortunate to have two people who love you so much." Again, Thomas hoped he had not destroyed Gloriana's love for him by how harshly he'd spoken to her. He couldn't imagine living without her. He refused to live without her!

"I have decided whatever goes on between you, Rowan, and Gloriana should not be my concern. I know my wife believes I can be unreasonable about men loving men." Gavin looked at Elizabeth, clearly wanting her to understand him. "It is not truly so. I simply do not encourage such actions, or desire for such actions to in any manner harm others. Such as James."

When he saw Thomas about to speak, he held up a hand to stop him. "I do not believe you would do anything to harm James."

Thomas felt a wave of relief at having the problem about Rowan finally settled. They did not flaunt their relationship in front of anyone, except for Gloriana. And she was now a big part of it. Still, there was something in Gavin's eyes that warned him matters about his son were far from settled. He grew tense again, held to his strained patience.

"Yet you do not want me to take James home with me to Middlemound," Thomas said it as a statement and not as a question. His stomach tightened as he waited for the other man's response.

Gavin jutted out his chin. "All of us in this room know that James is *not* really your son."

Thomas's nostrils flared. He dug his nails into the palms of his fisted hands. "He *is* my son and I have *always* claimed him. Mayhap I was unprepared until now to act his father, but he *is* my son."

He saw Elizabeth's eyes mist over and her lower lip tremble at his fierce declaration. Gavin held his gaze and said grimly, "All at Montrose know Sarah let another man into her bed when you were away. All know how few times you and she had relations. The people there have not seen James since he was but a babe, but they would see his blood father in him. Not your dark hair, not your blue eyes."

Thomas squared his shoulders, fought back his long-buried anger with his first wife. Times were difficult for them and between them. He had known about her cuckolding him. He could have stopped it, should have. But the past was the past. He could not change any of that.

"Sarah was *my* wife when she gave birth to James and died," he stated forcefully. "The true father cared nothing about his son, or about Sarah. I offered the man a horse for James, although I did not have to offer him anything. As her husband, I had the right to claim the boy."

He scowled in disgust, remembering the man's greed as he'd wanted more. Yet he'd settled for the horse and left. "He took the horse and gladly abandoned them both." Now tears silently trickled down Elizabeth's face. She nodded and said, "You know that he died shortly after leaving Montrose."

The man's death was the only one at his hands that didn't haunt Thomas. "I knew." Gavin gave him a simple nod. Thomas saw in his eyes that he knew what Thomas had done and approved.

"I do not think the boy knows for sure you are not his real father, though he might suspect. He is not a foolish lad." Gavin looked at Thomas, frowned. "I imagine he realizes he has not your hair or your eyes. And I was there one day not too far back when he asked Elizabeth about his mother. She told him of Sarah's dark hair and green eyes."

Elizabeth looked miserable. "I never realized … I did not mean to hurt him." She swallowed hard. "He has the blond hair of his true father and her green eyes."

Thomas tried to speak calmly in face of his sister's desolation. "What or who he looks like matters naught to me. James is my son. I will allow no one at either Montrose or Middlemound to question that."

Gavin nodded approval. "I believe after all of these years, Thomas, that you have finally become the man you were destined to be. Not the great warrior known by your reputation. But a man who can now settle and have a family."

He straightened, putting an arm around Elizabeth's shoulders to hold her to him. "I know of how you intend to train soldiers instead of going off to war. How Rowan will train them with you. These men will become the best in the land, I know this."

Thomas saw the admiration in the other man's face, but was surprised that Gavin knew of his plans. "How did—"

Gavin smiled. "I know many things. Another of which is that James deserves to have a man for a father who *chooses* him for a son." He nodded acceptance. "Your son is at my cousin's holding less than a day's ride from here." Thomas had hoped, certainly not expected, Abernon would meet him half way concerning either Rowan or James. He'd gone much farther. He stepped toward the man to shake his hand, but hesitated reaching out, uncertain because of his relationship with Rowan.

"Husband," Elizabeth encouraged, stepping away from him.

In the next second, Gavin put his arm out and they clasped forearms. "Will Rowan ride with you?" "Nay. I wish him to stay here with Gloriana. If tis all right with you."

He waited anxiously for his brother-in-law's agreement.

"He is welcome here."

***

Rowan had slept restlessly, still worried about Thomas for any number of reasons. He'd been here on the observation platform above the Abernon's keep for hours now. Dawn was threading pink and yellow colors through the spattering of clouds. At least the rain had finally stopped. He blamed riding for nearly four days through hit and miss rain for Thomas's illness. At least his friend had recovered well enough by last eve. *Thank God.* Yet he worried that Gloriana, too, might come down with whatever had felled her husband. She'd shown no signs of it, but he was in the mood to worry, he guessed. *About Thomas. About Gloriana. About them.*

He looked across the bailey and toward the miles of low, rolling hills beyond Abernon's walls. The area was nice, excellent for guarding this ancient fortress, with no forests to hide enemies. Still, he liked both Montrose and Middlemound better and was anxious to go home. Odd thought, that. *Home.* He couldn't remember when he'd actually thought about a "home." Now that he was aging—though only eight and twenty— he kind of liked the idea of spending more nights sleeping on a mattress than on the hard ground somewhere. He'd given little thought to more than having a regular place to lay his body down at night. Maybe someday he would. One step at a time, as Thomas had said recently.

He leaned forward to brace his forearms on the stone wall of the platform. Thomas had much on his mind these days. He'd adjusted fairly well to being married again, but that had much to do with Gloriana. From the times Thomas had talked about Sarah, he knew she was nothing like Glori. Sarah had played games with Thomas. He'd not really cared because he hadn't loved her and because he'd been gone so often from Montrose. Glori didn't try to manipulate anyone, at least not that Rowan was aware of.

It still sickened him to think about how Stewart had abused her. She could have remained beaten down by what had happened to her, could have become bitter, but she had blossomed in her growing love of Thomas. Rowan understood how it could happen. He, too, had suffered many abuses over the years and become resentful at times, leery of trusting anyone. He'd had many lovers—men as well as women—but only Thomas had found a way into his soul. He loved Thomas and for far more than just his body or his skills at lovemaking.

His body began its familiar thrumming of excitement when he thought about Thomas and the way they came together. Fiery came to mind. And now that Gloriana had shown a desire to join them, at least occasionally, the experience had become much hotter. She wanted a babe. Rowan heaved a frustrated sigh. He'd gladly give her one, but that truly wouldn't solve the problem. The problem was Thomas. And his fears. Those fears involved more than the possibility of her dying while giving birth. Thomas hadn't really said as much, but

Rowan suspected they were more tied to James.

*James.* Thomas was obsessed with this need to get his son back. Rowan imagined it had to do with his life being more settled. He had a holding in which he was content to stay. He no longer wished to go off and battle in every war and siege. And he had Gloriana, who would make a great mother to any child, in particular to James. But first Thomas had to make peace with Abernon.

Rowan's jaw hardened. *Abernon,* he knew by reputation, could be a loyal and tenacious warrior to have at your side. He could also be a formidable enemy. He saw things as right or wrong. Elizabeth had told them he didn't approve of men loving men, of the idea of him being with Thomas.

He shoved away from the wall and headed into the keep. It was time to find Abernon and have a hard talk with him. He prayed he could make the man see reason. But if he did not and their being together would keep Thomas from gaining his son, then Rowan would be forced to end their relationship. He loved both Thomas and Gloriana enough to walk away. Although he damn well didn't want to do so.

***

Rowan found Abernon breaking his fast with Elizabeth on the lord's raised dais at the front of the great hall. The room was nearly filled with soldiers, both Abernon's and Thomas's. Maids scurried from table to table bringing baskets of fresh breads, cheeses, pastries, and jugs of mead. Loud, boisterous chatter mixed with men teasing one another. A number of heads turned in his direction as he strode directly toward the lord of the castle.

"I need to talk to you when you are done. In private." Rowan had wanted to say "now," but contained his growing sense of urgency.

Elizabeth raised an eyebrow. "You seem distressed, Sir Rowan."

Abernon appeared to be studying him, although Rowan couldn't tell what the man was thinking. He felt uncomfortable, defensive. "Nay distressed, but the matter is important."

Surprising him, Abernon picked up a last bite of bread and pushed his chair back. He nodded toward the stairs. "We can talk in my solar." "Husband," Elizabeth said his name as if cautioning him about something. Worry creased her pretty face.

The hard warrior placed a big hand on his wife's shoulder and said quietly, "I know. Listen well. Judge wisely."

Rowan wondered at his words while he walked silently behind the man up to the solar on the second floor.

Abernon motioned Rowan into the large room containing a desk, a handful of wooden chairs near the scarred desk, and large tapestries of the castle itself and its heraldry. The room was lit by numerous torches. As Rowan walked across the room, Abernon asked, "What is so important this morn that you feel you must talk to me in private?" "Thomas. Me. Us." Rowan bit out the words, irritated that this was even necessary.

The slightly older man walked slowly around his desk and sat down in the chair behind it. He again seemed to study Rowan before saying, "By *us* I assume you are referring to the fact that you and Thomas are lovers."

Heat singed Rowan's face beneath his night's beard. He wasn't used to discussing his sexual relationships, although they generally didn't mean much to him. This one did. He'd been forewarned Abernon disapproved of men loving men. He'd been judged on the issue before. Before now, it hadn't mattered.

He moved to stand directly in front of Abernon, rigid, grim. "I will not deny that we are. But we keep our relations private. Neither of us wants others to feel uncomfortable because of our arrangement, because of our need for one another." Abernon raised an eyebrow. "Need?"

"Tis much the same fierce desire you feel for Elizabeth at times. Thomas and I are both very passionate men. Our needs are strong."

"I do not wish to know about your passions or your desires for one another." Abernon frowned, appeared almost angry and then he calmed. "I am well aware of your legends as a lover, Sir Rowan. With women as well as with men. A situation which puzzles me, since I thought ... well, that men who … who…"

Blowing out a breath of impatience, Rowan said, "Some of us who enjoy being with a man also enjoy being with a woman." Then he narrowed his eyes. "Thomas has only ever been with women. Until me. He does not have a fondness for admiring other men on occasion, as do I. Although I am no longer interested in other men, only in Thomas."

Abernon was quiet a minute, looked thoughtful. "How does Gloriana fit in your … your situation?" The man was clearly curious. "He appears to have strong feelings for her. As does she, for him."

This whole discussion was an uneasy one, though not as hard as he'd feared. It was difficult to stand and be judged by this stranger, by this man so important in Thomas's life at the moment. Rowan's stomach tightened from the stress of not miss-speaking. He wasn't sure what to say and decided to go with honesty. "Our Lady Gloriana was verbally and physically abused by her first husband. Both Thomas and I would gladly kill the man ourselves, if he were not already dead and, hopefully, rotting in Hell." Surprise and then anger flashed over Abernon's face. "Tis a sad matter. I'd heard Stewart was a vile man, knew he'd been her husband. But I … Anyway, I understand your feelings on the issue."

The man's words calmed Rowan a bit. Still, he thought it important for Abernon to learn more of the situation between Thomas and Gloriana. He sighed in resignation and proceeded. "Gloriana no sooner learned that Stewart had died in the last battle of the Crusades than she learned King Edward demanded she marry Thomas."

"Middlemound is an important holding for the crown.

"Aye, and Thomas wanted it, even though he also holds Montrose. But he was resistant to the idea of marrying again. Even with the horrors of her past, Gloriana is a rare woman. Beautiful. Strong of heart and loving. Stubborn now and then as well." He smiled. "Still, it hasn't taken my friend long to become very fond of Glori. In fact, I think he is in love with her."

He took a second before adding, "As am I. In truth, if I had met her before Thomas … and he was not part of my life … I might have pursued marriage to her myself."

Abernon's eyes widened. "You are in love with her?"

"I am in love with them *both.* Each of them satisfies needs I had not known I had; someone whom I trusted to guard my back, someone who did not judge me by my past, someone whose passions run as deep as mine. There are more reasons I value their friendships as much as their acceptance of me."

"I do not wish to know if the three of you have had relations together, though I suspect as much."

Although Abernon denied wanting to know, Rowan saw the interest in his eyes. But he was glad not to have to talk about that very private situation.

"Just how much are you willing to sacrifice for those you profess to love?" Abernon looked at Rowan pointedly. "Should I decide to keep James from Thomas unless you were out of their lives, would you leave?" He sat back, watching Rowan, studying him…judging him.

Rowan stiffened, fisted his hands at his sides. This was what he'd feared. And yet Abernon had not actually made a demand, he'd only proposed it as a question. Something seemed odd now. He'd expected more hostility from the man. He'd expected he might even have to physically defend himself, which had happened other times.

He looked Abernon straight in the eye. "If necessary, I would walk away from them both. Thomas needs his son in his life. Gloriana needs to act a mother, and James may be her only chance at that."

Abernon looked curious about that statement, but left it alone. Instead, he leaned forward and spoke even more seriously. "James is not Thomas's son." Again, the man seemed to study him, intent on how Rowan reacted.

Rowan hadn't known for sure that James had another father, but he'd suspected as much. It mattered naught to Thomas, so it mattered naught to Rowan. "In all ways that matter, he is."

He was a bastard himself, even if the Duke had claimed him. James was lucky to have been claimed by a good man such as Thomas. "A father is more than a man who spills his seed in a woman to get her with child."

To his surprise, Abernon nodded. "I know your father." The tightness in his expression said the man did not like the Duke of Remington.

Neither said more on the subject.

"As I have already told Thomas, what you and he, and Gloriana, have together is none of my concern."

"*Already told Thomas?*" Rowan asked in confusion. Had the man gone to Thomas's chamber and discussed this with his friend while he was still recovering from illness? "Nay, I did not go to him on the matter, if that is what you are thinking." Abernon sat back in his chair. "He came to my bedchamber early this morning, demanding we talk, which we did. He is gone now. Thomas left over an hour ago for my cousin's holding, to get James, with my approval."

Rowan blinked in surprise and then grumbled under his breath, "I should have gone with him." Abernon shook his head. "Thomas wanted you to stay here to watch after Gloriana. I do not think he totally trusts me. But he did take two of his men with him. They should be back on the morrow, if James gives him no problems."

Something worried Rowan, something he felt deep in his gut. *Trouble of some kind.* It had been a long time since he hadn't guarded Thomas's back. He didn't like the situation at all.

"I would feel better being at his side." Gloriana would be all right here. His gut knew that as well. "I trust you will watch after our lady."

"*Your* lady?" Abernon asked with a raised eyebrow, though he gave a nod of agreement.

"Aye, *our* lady. Thomas knows my feelings are strong for her. He also knows I would never overstep what boundaries we set for one another." He felt an urgency that was driving him from the keep. "Watch after her."

He strode out of the room, heading for the paddocks.

***

Gloriana sat in the middle of the rumpled bed where she'd been sitting, thinking, and crying ever since Thomas had left in anger. She was more than tired of acting this way. Yet she couldn't seem to make herself get up and dress.

She heard a tap on the closed chamber door and started. Thomas would surely not knock, even if he knew she was angry with him. Rowan might, but she didn't think it was him there either. Who else could it be?

Elizabeth's worried voice called out, "Gloriana? May I speak with you?"

"A moment," Gloriana said. She scrambled off the bed and quickly pulled the gown she'd worn yesterday over her head. She'd get the other woman to fasten up the back. "Come in."

As Elizabeth walked in and seemed to try not to look at the bed,

Gloriana felt embarrassed. The scent of lovemaking was still in the air. Her gown was rumpled, and she awkwardly clasped it together behind her back with one hand. Her cheeks flamed.

Before she could say anything, Elizabeth walked behind her and began lacing up the back of her dress. "I was worried about you. But I suspected you were sleeping in after so many long hours tending to Thomas."

As soon as her dress was laced up, Gloriana walked to her trunk and pulled out the brush. Elizabeth looked as perfectly groomed as the lady of the manor should. A fact that made Gloriana feel incompetent as this lady's sister-in-law. She was a disaster, from not having been properly dressed, to no doubt having red blotches from crying on her face. Which, thankfully, Elizabeth had not commented upon.

She turned away, hoping her face would clear while she brushed at her long hair. "Aye, I am slow in getting around this morn." Then trying to keep her tone casual, she asked, "Have you spoken to Thomas already? I really should go down to speak with him as well." She lowered her voice and said awkwardly, "We had some words."

"He said as much when he came to our chamber early this morn. He seemed very distressed about it."

Gloriana heard the concern in Elizabeth's tone and turned, no longer caring if the other woman saw the results of her bout with crying. She watched Elizabeth sit on the side of the bed and fidget to smooth her skirt. "You will forgive him, will you not? Thomas loves you," Elizabeth said, her expression worried.

The brush stilled in Gloriana's hair. "He has never actually said that." She knew it, though, in her heart.

"Men can be foolish sometimes." Elizabeth lightly laughed. "All right, more than sometimes. Quite often actually."

The door was still open and Gavin walked inside. "Watch what you say, wife," he chided, yet Gloriana saw tenderness in his eyes.

"Do you follow me, my lord?"

"All the rest of the days of my life." He blushed and seemed to realize they weren't alone. He straightened and looked to Gloriana. "I need to speak with you."

Gloriana's heart fluttered. The man really was rather intimidating, even when he wasn't frowning. "About what, Lord Abernon?"

Elizabeth watched him, appeared to give him a look of warning.

"Why do you keep doing that this morn? Have I yet harmed anyone? Have I even yelled at anyone?" he asked in disgruntlement.

He faced Gloriana again. "I wish to talk to you about Thomas and Rowan."

She stiffened and lowered the hairbrush, holding it tightly. "Elizabeth has already told us that you know they are lovers. It is not for *you* to judge them. They are good men, respected warriors, loyal to the king."

The side of his mouth twitched. "You are as fiercely loyal to them as they are to each other. And to you."

She blinked at him. "You have spoken to them? This morn?"

"Aye. Separately. Each demanded to talk with me. In truth, it has been a long time since anyone has shown me such loyalty. I cannot help but respect them."

He moved to stand beside his wife. "Tis a complicated situation you are part of, Lady Middlemound."

Gloriana nodded and gave a small sigh. "Aye. Loving two strong-headed men can be quite a..." She slammed her mouth shut and gaped at them. Elizabeth smiled and Abernon nodded. "As I said, my lady, a complicated situation. More than I would choose to deal with. Although it still surprises me, I do not have an issue with it."

She breathed a sigh of relief. Then her thoughts turned to Thomas and James. "You will try to keep James from coming with us? Because of..."

He shook his head. "Nay. My reason for being wary of letting Thomas take James was because the boy is not his true son. I did not want the boy hurt more than he has already been."

"Not his 'true son'?" Gloriana looked from Gavin to Elizabeth. "I do not understand."

Elizabeth put a hand to her husband's leg and said, "Let me explain."

She met Gloriana's eyes and seemed to study her for a few seconds. "When my brother was away from Montrose, Sarah took other men to her bed. One man in particular. Thomas knew this and yet did not attempt to stop her. He simply did not care."

Gloriana knew he hadn't loved Sarah, and she clearly hadn't loved him. But to hurt him like that. She curled her hand around the brush in anger. "So James is the other man's son?"

Abernon took over, his mouth tight in displeasure. "Aye. You need not know all that happened, just that the other man is dead. He was never in James's life, never wanted to be."

"Poor James. Poor Thomas," Gloriana said quietly, her heart aching for them both. "My brother claimed James from the second of his birth. It has never mattered to him whose seed he was born of." Elizabeth wiped at a tear. "Thomas can be a fearsome man at times, but he cares deeply about many things. He did not know what to do with a babe. He was a warrior. Without a wife and a real home, he believed he had nothing to offer his son. So he gave him to Gavin and me to raise until he was ready to act the father. It was never that he wished to deny the boy, or not love him." Gloriana thought about the sadness she saw in her husband's eyes at times. The longing she saw in them as well when he talked about James. She looked at Elizabeth. "He believes he has failed as a father until now. He needs to see if he can be one. That is why..."

Elizabeth frowned. "Why what?"

"Why he has been refusing to give me a babe," Gloriana admitted and the last of her anger with him faded away. Somehow they would get through all of this. She would help him be the father he wanted to be.

"God's teeth, I shall have to box his ears when he returns." Elizabeth pursed her lips, looking furious.

"When he returns?" Gloriana asked, worry curling through her. "He went to get James, didn't he? Alone, I suppose."

"He took two of his men when he rode out just after dawn," Abernon countered. "When Rowan and I finished talking a short while ago, he went after your husband. He felt some kind of urgency to catch up with him. Rowan muttered something about a bad feeling as he left the solar."

Her stomach clenched. *Rowan had a bad feeling? About Thomas? Oh, dear God!* She was about to question Abernon further when footsteps pounded up the stairs. She tensed, waiting.

One of Thomas's men hurried into the open doorway and looked anxiously at her. He barely glanced at Abernon and Elizabeth. His expression warned her of something bad.

"Thomas?" she questioned in dread. The man shook his head.

"Nay, my lady, it is Sir Rowan." He drew in a breath as if deciding what to say to her. Gloriana dropped the hairbrush, took a step toward him. Her voice trembled with fear as she asked, "What? What about Rowan?" "He has been badly hurt. You must come quickly."

## Chapter Ten

Gloriana raced out of the keep, heart pounding, tears misting her eyes. She blinked them away and looked to the paddock where Thomas's men ringed the first of the three paddocks. Tension sizzled in the air. She could almost smell their anger, their outrage. Many had their hands on the hilts of their swords. Others held sharp and deadly knives. Gavin's men stood looking equally hostile, just as heavily armed only a few feet away. She heard fierce curses and bitter grumblings, but at least for the moment they were not attacking one another. She cared for none of this. Her sole focus was to get to Rowan.

"My lady, wait," the soldier who had come to tell her the news called to her, desperate.

"Nay!" She moved faster, determined he not stop her. She heard Gavin's heavy steps behind the soldier, growing closer as well. And Elizabeth's lighter steps, too. But she would not be kept from getting to Rowan.

She shoved between Gavin's men. Though one dared to grab her arm to stop her, she glowered up at him in such fury that he released her and stepped out of her path. Thomas's men saw her coming, saw her determination, and moved aside to allow her into the paddock. As she passed between them, she caught the angered comments about how some of Gavin's soldiers had been lying in wait for Rowan. How they'd attacked him. She also heard praise for how he'd been outnumbered, without weapons, and yet had fought fiercely. Her heart raced with dread and tears threatened once more. *Dear God, why had this happened?* Gloriana looked into the dimly lit area, searching frantically for Rowan. Three dead men lay in the bloody straw, blood draining from numerous knife wounds. She gaped, held her stomach, nearly gagged but fought it back. These men had died hard, but she had no sympathy for them.

She swallowed hard. *Blood, blood, blood.* It seemed to be everywhere. She smelled the sickening sweet scent and her stomach threatened to heave again. She could not give in to weakness! *Where was Rowan?*

Then she heard a low moan not far away. Her heart pounded. *Please, please let me be in time to save him.*

She spotted him lying at the back wall, braced against it, an arm crossed over his ribs. He breathed slowly in and out. He seemed to moan more with each breath. She ached for him, with him.

As she approached him, Rowan raised a bloodied knife in defense. But when he recognized her, his gaze settled on her through the slit of one of his swollen eyes. He lowered the knife. A shudder of relief passed over him. "Glori." It was all he could manage to say before grimacing.

Before either of them could draw in another breath, Gloriana was on her knees in the straw beside him. She noted his many bloody wounds, and saw the tender way he held his ribs. Tears streamed down her cheeks. His dear face had been beaten so badly. His nose had bled profusely, looked slightly bent and was no doubt broken. A knife slash ran down the left side of his face and seeped blood. The slash had barely missed his eye, though fists had pounded that eye and the other one. His lips were swollen as well, cracked on one side and bleeding. It hurt her to even look at him.

Blinking back tears, she tried to look around where he held tight to his obviously bruised, possibly broken ribs. A long slash cut his tunic on the left side and blood soaked through from the wound. Another slash ran at an angle over his right thigh, blood seeping out there as well through his now dirty braies. He'd been mercilessly beaten and forced to defend himself in a knife battle. He could have died, but he was a fierce fighter. He would never die easily. She thanked God for that.

"Oh, Rowan," she said in a tortured whisper. She reached to gently touch the side of his battered face. "Why would someone…"

Her question was cut off when Gavin stormed up behind her, Elizabeth, too. Gavin swore at what he saw and Gloriana felt his fury, though it didn't come close to matching her own.

Rowan stiffened in distress, groaning, tried to focus on her and Gavin. "They…were waiting…for me," he said in between ragged breaths. "were doing…Gavin's bidding."

Gloriana immediately turned a murderous look at Gavin. "Is this true, Lord Abernon?"

Before he could defend himself, Rowan grunted out, "Not believe them."

He sucked in a pain-filled breath. "I killed one." Another pained breath. "Gavin's first knight…came to…help me." He closed his eyes and grimaced. "He killed…the other two."

Gloriana saw Gavin curl his hands into fists. "I would never condone this kind of attack. If those men were not already dead, I would hang them this day."

Even though it was clear any kind of movement cost him, Rowan gave a weak nod. "Good man. Your first knight, too." "We need to get you inside," Gloriana said, desperate to begin tending to his wounds. Yet she knew moving him in any manner now would hurt him.

"Nay. Leave here," Rowan said grimly. "Today." He tried to move only to fall back cursing. "Cannot endanger…you…Thomas."

"You *are* safe here, Sir Rowan," Gavin bit out. "I will kill with my own hand any who would dare to try something like this again."

Elizabeth put a gentle hand on his arm, but her husband didn't calm down. Gloriana could tell that this attack had made him far beyond angry. A guest in his home had been beaten. If he hadn't been a seasoned warrior, Rowan would have been killed. She understood his fury, felt it herself.

Her focus returned to Rowan. Gloriana knew without further explanations that he'd been attacked by men who hated the idea of him being a lover of men. His emotional suffering would be great, too, from this. She wanted to pull him against her chest and coddle him like a child who had been injured. She wanted to soothe his many aches and pains. But he was a man, a hardened warrior. His pride ran deeper than that of most men. He would only allow so much soothing and tender ministrations. She would give him all that he would allow.

"Cannot stay," Rowan repeated, struggling for breath.

Everything in her wanted to scream out in outrage. But this was not the time for losing control. He needed her to be strong now. She looked up to Elizabeth. "Have water, ale, rags, and medicinals brought to me. I will clean and wrap his wounds as best I can here."

Then she shifted her gaze to Gavin. "I would ask to have a wagon prepared that I can borrow and in which I can take Rowan to Montrose."

"He can heal here. He will be safe here," Gavin protested, although he didn't sound angry at her request.

"You must…stay here…wait for Thomas." Rowan looked anxiously at her, or as best he could with such a battered face. "He expects…"

She raised her chin and refused to back down. "He expected you to stay here while he went to get James, wanted you to watch after me. I know this. I know his thinking. If he knew you had been hurt, he would expect me to care for you. I know this as well." "Why can you not tend to his wounds here? Let Sir Rowan heal here?" Elizabeth asked, sounding worried. "Thomas's own men can guard his chamber."

"Because he wishes to leave." Gloriana sensed Rowan needed to be away from here. He no doubt worried that no matter how much Gavin said nothing like this would happen again, it could. Or that someone would harm her. And he wasn't in a condition to defend himself and certainly not her. She would do whatever necessary to give him some peace of mind. "We will leave as soon as the wagon is ready and I have cleansed these wounds." Gavin nodded in understanding, gave her a tight smile. "Thomas has found himself a stubborn woman, like my Elizabeth. You will do well together." His gaze shifted to Rowan. "All of you will."

***

The trip to Alexander Campbell's castle hadn't been an easy one. Thomas's body had still been healing, but he'd been too restless to take any longer to go after James. And he'd been ready to get all of this matter behind him. Now that Gavin apparently backed him, Thomas felt more confident that he could, in fact, be a good father to James. He didn't care about whether or not the boy was from his loins. The boy needed to know he was loved, know that there would always be someone there for him. Of course, Gavin and Elizabeth would fill that role if needed, but it wasn't the same. James needed a father. Thomas wanted to be that father.

He glanced over at the boy riding stoically on the horse next to him. The initial meeting between them two days earlier hadn't gone well. James had not wanted to come with him, had not wanted to go anywhere with him. Ever. "You do not really want me. You never have." The boy's words had been spoken bitterly, and Thomas had felt the pain behind them. Yet somehow, at some point, Thomas had managed to say something that had gotten through James's defenses. He still wasn't sure what he'd said. He was only grateful to have convinced his son to give him a chance.

"Gloriana has a soft woman's heart," Thomas said, thinking once more about how anxious he was to get back to her. They had much making up to do. *He* had much making up to do. He'd hurt her and he hated that.

James thrust his chin up. “I need no softness.” Thomas heard the years of longing for a real mother in those bitten-out words. His son wanted exactly that, but, like himself, he didn’t want to admit it. He trusted his wife to find her own way with the boy. “Mayhap *you* do not. But she is a gentle person, and you will not hurt her tender feelings.”

“Why would she want anything to do with me?” James asked, sounding defensive and yet hopeful. “She is not my true mother.” He looked narrowly at Thomas. “*You* are not my true father.”

“We have had this discussion, about my being your father. I will not deal with it again. You *are* my son. No one will ever challenge that.” When he saw the boy’s cautious acceptance, knew the hope he held inside him, Thomas softened. It angered him that he’d taken this long to do the right thing by James. “Gloriana loves children, has already said she will love you like her own.” Again, he caught the desperate need to be truly loved on James’s face before he tried to cover it. “When you get her with child, she will forget about me. *You* will forget about me.” James looked straight ahead at the outer walls of Abernon as they rode steadily closer.

*When he got her with child.* The look of devastation on her face at his cruelty before he’d left the bedchamber still haunted Thomas. She’d stopped drinking the tea. She could even now be with child. He no longer feared that. Now that he was making good progress with James, he knew they would be all right. He could be a good father. Not perfect, but better than many. He *would* be better than many, certainly better than his own father. And he would like to see a little girl with blonde hair and green eyes running about Middlemound. She would be a trial just like her mother. He wanted that. He smiled. “Gloriana has enough love in her heart for you, me, and many more children.” He looked directly at James. “You will always be my firstborn son. I will never forget you. I have never forgotten you.”

James gave a timid nod of acceptance, and they continued quietly, almost comfortably, toward Abernon.

***

From the moment Thomas rode into Abernon’s front bailey he knew something was wrong. He led the two men he’d taken with him and James toward the keep’s steps. It was mid-day and the bailey should have been filled with men practicing and villagers bustling about. Instead there were only a dozen or so men in the side bailey, none were his soldiers.

He glanced to the men with him and said warily, "Stay here. I need to find Lord Abernon and Sir Rowan."

Gavin walked from around the side of the keep before he could dismount. The minute he spotted Thomas his expression grew grave. He walked determinedly closer as Thomas's stomach tensed. "Gloriana?" He feared something had happened to her. He didn't know why that was his first thought, but it was. He knew without a doubt now that he loved her. "Come, talk with me," Gavin motioned him over and moved farther away again.

Thomas didn't like this at all, but he quickly slid from his horse and followed his brother-in-law. He still wondered why he'd not seen his other men come out to greet him, or Rowan. It was past the noon meal, yet they could be inside the keep.

"Gloriana and Rowan are not here, neither are most of your men," Gavin said. His brow furrowed and he looked uneasily toward the paddocks. "Rowan was attacked by three men—now all dead—the day you left to get James. He had intended to go catch up with you."

Thomas stiffened, could barely breathe. "Attacked?" Then he gasped, "Is he…is he dead?" *God, please no!*

Gavin shook his head, though his expression remained serious. "Nay, at least I do not believe so. If he were not such a hardy warrior, he would have died as he fought back."

Thomas felt a second of relief. Until he latched onto the words "I do not believe so" and remembered Gavin also saying that Gloriana and Rowan weren't here. He scowled at Gavin. "You sent them away," he accused.

Fury was crawling through him. Somehow he knew in his gut why his friend had been attacked. If the men weren't already dead, he would hunt them down and… But they were dead. Still, it tore at him that he hadn't been here to defend Rowan. And Gavin had…

Before Thomas could do more than fist his hands in anger, Gavin shook his head. "Nay, I did naught." He jutted out his chin and stood ready to defend himself if necessary. "I told them to stay here and wait for you. I would have protected them. I would naught have let such a thing happen again." He was all but growling in his frustration. "I have talked to all of my men about the matter. All know I will naught tolerate such actions here." Thomas sucked in steadying breaths while Gavin looked squarely at him. Gavin added in disgust, "In truth, the men who attacked your friend were new here, drunk. Neither of which are tolerable excuses. I would have hung them, but Rowan managed to kill one. My first knight killed the other two when he went to help your friend."

*Died. Rowan could have died.* Thomas had trouble absorbing the news. He pushed the thought aside for now. He needed to go after his wife and the man he loved. He needed to see for himself that they were all right. And he needed to hold them both. "Where have they gone?"

"Rowan wanted to go to Montrose." When Thomas started to move back toward his horse, Gavin stopped him. "You should know that he wanted Gloriana to stay here. I think he believed it might be best if he—"

Thomas rounded on him, anger flaring within him. "I know what he would have thought. Foolish man!" He blew out a ragged breath. "I ask that you keep James here while I go settle matters with my wife and Rowan. We will come back for him as soon as possible."

Gavin nodded, although he looked uncertain about Thomas's plan.

Thomas didn't want to leave James again. He'd worked hard to make what little progress he had with his son. But what if more danger lay waiting for Rowan at Montrose? They had not expected anything to happen here at Abernon, other than possibly having to make war against his brother-in-law to regain his son. What if someone at Montrose were of like mind to those who had attacked Rowan here? Not the men he and Rowan had battled beside, men they both trusted with their backs. But there had been some men at Montrose that were new. What if... *No. He must check out the situation before he took his son into such a possibly volatile situation.*

Feeling yet another heavy burden on his shoulders, Thomas said with determination, "I will talk to James. I will make him understand that I am not abandoning him again. I will come back for him. Soon."

***

Rowan paced his bedchamber, stopping to look out the narrow window at the people below in the bailey. More men than normal were working out in the practice field. Montrose soldiers and Middlemound soldiers. The Middlemound soldiers should have been waiting at Abernon for Thomas's return with James. But when Rowan had insisted on coming here to Montrose to heal from the attack, Gloriana had insisted on coming with him. Which meant that her husband's soldiers insisted on escorting her. He didn't want all of these people around. He wanted to get over his wounds and deal with the attack on his own. It hadn't been the first time someone had attacked him for his sexual habits. But it had been the first time he'd actually come close to being killed. As much as that bothered him, it worried him more that his choices would one day bring harm to Thomas or to Gloriana. He could not live with himself if anything happened to either of them. He needed to end this between them. Somehow.

*Gloriana. God's teeth, she was a stubborn woman.* She'd barely left his side in the two days they been here. If she wasn't fussing over one of his wounds, she was trying to talk to him. She wanted to make sure he was all right, emotionally as well as physically. Women didn't understand that men didn't talk about their feelings. He knew she meant well, but he was going crazy. She needed Thomas and James to worry over, not him. His stomach was beginning to growl, a sign that he was finally healing. He'd eaten very little since his arrival here. Another matter which upset Gloriana. She had insisted he needed to eat to regain his strength, but his jaw had been too sore to chew. She'd wanted him to eat broths then. Even with that he'd struggled. He couldn't open his mouth wide enough for the spoon. Actually the efforts had been wasted anyway. He'd been nauseous until only this morn. Now he could move his jaw better, and the smells of cooking beef and fresh bread drifting up through the keep made him hungry.

Rowan heaved a sigh of frustration. Hungry or not, he was reluctant to leave this chamber. He didn't want to see the sympathetic looks on the faces of Thomas's men again. He didn't want pity. But staying here until the bruises fully faded in mayhap two weeks was a foolish idea. He was not a coward. It was time to forget his wounded pride and find the strength to bend enough to pull on his braies. Damn ribs. Even climbing from the bed to walk around or to use the chamber pot hurt like Hell.

Before he could turn from the window to seek his clothes, there was a familiar tap on his chamber door. *Gloriana.* He froze, caught standing naked. From experience, he knew she didn't have much patience. She would knock once more and then she would walk into the room. She didn't put up with his attempts to ignore her.

He gingerly started toward the bed. "Come back later, Glori," he called out.

"Nay, you are not going to send me away again." He'd done so already twice this morn and she hadn't been happy about it. "I have brought you some honey mead." "Glori—" But she shoved the big wooden door open and his words faded away as she gaped at him.

He was normally not a shy man in front of a woman, but this was their Glori. This was different. She wasn't seeing him at his best. He watched her eyes tear up as she looked at his battered body. His bruises were better each day. His jaw less swollen. But he had a new bend to his nose. He was dealing with it, had dealt with much worse. Gloriana had nursed him and seen all of his injuries, but it still bothered her tender heart to see him like this. He knew this because she'd admitted it time and again.

When her gaze shifted downward to his abdomen and then moved even lower to the bandage on his thigh, he had a problem. She'd barely glanced at his semi-hard cock before it had sprung to attention.

"You should have come back, Glori," he grumbled and slowly walked to the bed. He carefully sat down and pulled the bed linen over his lower body. It tented over his erection.

Heat spread up her face, but she stepped into the chamber and pushed the door closed with her hip. "You have nothing today that I have not seen before." She marched across the room and handed him the mug of mead. "Tis good to see you up and about. Would you like me to help you dress? You could mayhap go downstairs for the nooning meal."

Rowan shook his head. "Nay, you will not help me dress."

Now that he was healing, he didn't think he could stand having her touch him in any manner again. She smelled too good, like she'd taken a bath this morn and used that flowery soap she favored. She looked too good, slim and yet her plump breasts nearly spilled from the low neckline. He wanted to cup them with his hands. He wanted to put his mouth over the nipples. In truth, he longed to strip her of the green gown and see her naked body. And he wanted to feel that lusciously, soft naked body moving over him.

"You need to leave. While you can." His breaths were becoming ragged, which made his tender ribs hurt. "It has been too long since…" Since his body had found relief. Since Thomas had taken him and since he'd feasted on her.

She watched him, cocked her head and her long braid swung to one side. "You are not healed enough for too much movement, Rowan. Even were Thomas here, I could not allow you to take him…or him to bend you over to drive into your ass."

Now that she'd given him the image, he desperately wanted to bend over the bed's edge or go to all fours on the bed. He ached to have Thomas fill him with his long, thick cock. But she was right; such positions would cause him great pain. His ribs were far too unhealed for that. Nor could he bend Thomas over and ram into his ass. These were all depressing thoughts. Yet his cock remained hard.

"I could give you relief," she said quietly. "I do not like to see you suffer."

He followed her gaze to where his cock had pushed aside the bed linen, to where it boldly waved at her. As much as the idea intrigued him, he was still uncomfortable with the thought of any kind of sex with Thomas's wife. At least without his lover's permission.

Rowan reached to encircle his shaft with one hand, stroking it. "I can take care of my problem, my lady." But he ached to feel her sweet lips on him now. He stroked his shaft again. It was not the same as having someone's warm mouth working over him. He gave a small sigh of disappointment.

To his surprise, she walked determinedly toward him. "Thomas would not like to see you suffering. Or have me suffering, either." She held his gaze.

"I need to touch you." He saw how her eyes had darkened, how her nostrils flared as she drew in the scent of his arousal. "But I know you are resistant to being inside my body without Thomas approving. I love you even more for your loyalty to him."

*She loved him?* Aye, he knew that was true, had seen it in her gentle ways with him, in her insistence on caring for him. But he also knew she was in love with Thomas, no matter how he'd hurt her with his attitude about having a baby. And she was *his* legal wife. They could be lovers, but only with Thomas present and being a part of what they did.

"I love you, too, Glori." His hand stilled on his shaft. His pulse raced as she drew closer. "I love Thomas as well, this you know. I would never hurt him."

"Nor would I. There is much to work out between him and me, but it will be done. I can be patient with him for now." She had almost made it to the side of the bed when the door opened. Thomas stood silently for a long minute in the doorway. Rowan tensed.

What had he heard? What did he see now? A friend who was struggling not to betray him with his wife? A wife trying not to betray her husband?

"Thomas, I…" He didn't know what to say.

Thomas's expression filled with anger. He stepped into the room and firmly closed the door behind him, locked it, shoving the bar across the doorframe. As Gloriana stood very still and breathing shallowly next to him, Rowan waited for the feel of Thomas's fist to his tender jaw. He deserved whatever the man gave him. He'd found him naked in the room with his wife, granted it was Rowan's room and she was fully dressed.

"You will *not* remove yourself from our lives! Certainly not without discussing it first." Thomas strode right in front of Rowan and glowered down at him. "What happened was terrible, and I would kill the men given the chance. But it is not so terrible that I want you out of my life." He glanced toward his wife. "Or out of Glori's. She loves you. I love you. *We* love you."

Rowan felt relief wash over him. "I will not bring harm to you and your family." Even as he said the words, he couldn't stand the idea of not being with them.

"You are part of our family," Thomas gritted out as he leaned down. He gently cupped Rowan's face and kissed him. He deepened the kiss until Rowan heard the rapidness of his breathing before Thomas pulled away. "Do you understand now?" His cut lip ached from the pressure of Thomas's mouth against his. And as his heart pounded beneath his bruised ribs, he didn't care about the pain. "Aye."

Thomas turned to Gloriana and pulled her against him. His large hands smoothed over her braid. For a second he seemed content just to hold her. Then he kissed her with every bit the passion as he'd kissed Rowan.

She looked a bit dazed when Thomas released her. Rowan knew that feeling. Thomas was one hell of a kisser. His cock throbbed and he stroked it, drawing Thomas's attention. The anger in his expression was gone now, replaced by concern.

"Are you all right now, my friend?" Thomas asked, studying every inch of Rowan's body that he could see, including the way he stroked his cock.

Rowan decided to be honest. "I will be in time." Thomas nodded his understanding. He watched Rowan's hand on his shaft and turned to Gloriana. "He needs relief, as you said. But he cannot find it as we normally do. I cannot allow him to risk further injury."

"I can…" She began and then blushed. "Well, I can do what I have seen Rowan do to you. Or at least I can try."

"And I will take you, wife, as you please Rowan." He looked heatedly at them both. "Rowan, lie back in your bed. Glori, you will remove your gown and your chemise." With a smile, she gave him her back and said, "You will untie my laces, my lord." She focused on Rowan. "You are all right with this plan? You trust that I will not hurt you with my inexperience?"

Rowan's chest ached from the way his heart continued to pound with his desire. He was pretty sure there would be some pain for him as they moved over him on the bed, but he didn't care. He would have her sweet, warm mouth on him. He would have those plump breasts rubbing against him. And he could watch his lover drive into her body.

He looked from her to Thomas and knew his friend understood his thoughts. When he gave a small nod of approval, Rowan relaxed even more. "You will not hurt me, my lady. This I trust."

It took him a few minutes to ease back to the mattress and recover enough so he could breathe right. During that time, he watched them undress. A sight he would remember for a long time.

Gloriana trembled with excitement at the thought of what they were about to do together. This would be so much more than last time. She would get to actively participate. Yet as she watched Rowan carefully ease back onto the bed, she worried about him. Should they really be doing this now? While she'd been considering only moments ago giving him relief this way, now she wasn't sure. She didn't know what she was doing. Would she hurt him more?

She glanced uncertainly back at Thomas, who took her breath away just looking at him. All of that scarred but otherwise perfect man belonged to her. His hair was loose and she really wanted to touch it, run her fingers through the dark, thickness of it. His eyebrows were slightly pinched. She knew without him saying anything that he was distressed over what had happened to Rowan, concerned about how stiffly his friend moved, how bruised and battered he still looked. She wanted to smooth a finger along those eyebrows and along his brow, as if that could take away some of his worry. And, my oh my, she longed to press her body against his and kiss him. She wanted him to kiss her back like he'd done a few minutes ago. Only for far longer.

Breathing unsteadily, her gaze moved to the powerful rod standing tall and proud. Soon, blessedly soon, he would drive it inside of her.

She really, really wanted that. When he'd left her that horrible morn at Abernon, he'd been so angry with her. She'd been angry and hurt, too. So much had happened since then. She'd learned things she wished he would have shared with her so she could have understood him better. But her husband knew far more about how to war than how to love or how to share himself. She would teach him.

"Glori, are you all right?" Thomas finally asked. He cupped the side of her face, and she saw the concern in his eyes. Heat seared her from where he touched her to her woman's place. Her heart fluttered as did everything within her. "I do not wish to hurt Rowan. What if I do something wrong?"

Thomas's eyes darkened in desire and in tenderness. "Trust your instincts, my love. This is a precious gift you give our Rowan."

"Mayhap we should not do this," Rowan protested and drew their attention.

"Aye, we should." Thomas gave her an encouraging look and turned her toward the bed. "She loves you enough to do this."

Still a little nervous, Gloriana crawled slowly over the bed and between Rowan's slightly spread legs. He watched her, gave her a tiny nod of approval. She focused on his shaft and her heart fluttered even faster. Impressive, like Thomas's. Big, thick, tempting. Her mouth watered and warmth built low in her body.

"Thomas is right. I do love you. It pleases me that you allow me to do this for you." She touched his cock lightly with her fingers. The skin was soft, yet the thickness hard. She tapped her fingers ever so slowly up the length and smiled at how it jerked beneath her touch. Then she put her fingers around him, Rowan sucked in a breath. Immediately she looked up and found his face strained. "Have I done something wrong? Have I hurt you?"

"Nay, Glori." She sensed Thomas moving behind her and grew tense as well. As he put his hands on her bare buttocks, she quivered with awareness. Her hand tightened around Rowan's rod.

Rowan gently chastised, "Have a care, my lady."

Gloriana eased up, blushing. "Sorry. Tis Thomas's fault."

Thomas ignored her comment, instead saying, "Touch your tongue to the side of Rowan's shaft. Lick slowly along the veins."

Her whole body shivered at the huskiness in his tone yet she obeyed. As her tongue touched Rowan, he tensed, except for his shaft, which pulsed within her hold. She drew her tongue slowly along the side of the shaft, hearing his indrawn breath. But it was hard to concentrate on what she was doing. Thomas had reached a hand between her legs and started dragging a long finger over her swelling lower lips. She shivered from it.

"Put your mouth over the head of his cock," Thomas instructed huskily. "Swirl your tongue around it."

With a glance at Rowan to be sure he was still all right, Gloriana held the shaft near the base and opened her mouth wide enough to put it over the head. She inhaled the scent of his arousal, heard his groan of "Oh God!" and took in the wonder of the experience.

She'd barely dealt with that wonder when Thomas's finger slipped into her body, and then a second finger. Her body adjusted, wanted more. This time, his thumb found her pulsing bud and lightly flicked it.

"Ohhhh!" she gasped and pushed back, wanting still more of the pleasure swirling through her.

"You are ready, wife." Thomas announced, sounding pleased.

He put a hand to her back and gently pushed her lower, caused her bottom to lift higher. Then he guided his rod to the place so desperate for him. Again he gave her instructions; again his voice was thick with emotion. "You will take Rowan's shaft into your mouth as much as you can. Move it up and down his length. Massage him with your cheek muscles. Do whatever you are comfortable with."

She pulled her mouth free for a second to look back at her husband. The sight of him holding her hips, seeing that his rod was between her legs, and feeling it nudge at her entrance had her whole body trembling. "You will pound into me at the same time? As you do with Rowan?"

"Nay. Rowan is tougher and can take a fierce pounding." She watched Thomas's chest shudder, saw the tension in his face. "I will drive into you, but with more gentleness." Gloriana frowned. "Mayhap I would like more than gentleness."

Rowan snorted and drew a frown from her as well. "You are our lady, Glori. We will make passionate love to you, but we will never—"

Annoyed, she lightly bit the head of his cock.

He gave a surprised yelp.

Thomas smacked her bottom. "Have a care with him." He drove into her.

She arched backward and held her breath in reaction. *Yes, this is what she wanted.* "This pleases you?" He pulled nearly out and drove deep again.

"Oh aye!" She felt so full. Her inner muscles trembled with each deep drive.

Then she needed more, more of everything. She leaned down and found Rowan's shaft once more. She surrounded it with her hand, stroked it up and down at the same time Thomas rammed in and out of her body.

She took Rowan's rod into her mouth and sucked on it, breathing hard as she did so. She pulled her mouth up and down, her teeth lightly moving over the length. She swirled her tongue over the tip, around the head. All the while, he clutched at the bed linen and groaned. He lifted his body toward her, desperate for her to take him to that place he needed to find. At the same time, Thomas held tightly to her hips, kept her bent over with a hand to her back. He drove his cock steadily into her, gave her no mercy…nor did she want any. He panted behind her, grunted. The sounds were music to her ears. She was surrounded by the melodies of her men working hard to reach that magical place. One grunted, one groaned. One moaned, one panted.

Finally, sounding almost wild, Rowan shot his seed down her throat. She struggled to swallow it and looked up in concern at him. She needed to know he was all right, that what she'd done hadn't hurt him. His cries had been of pain, but the clear satisfaction now in his gaze, made her relax.

Now she was free to rest her head against Rowan's stomach and enjoy the firestorm Thomas was building within her. He clutched her hips so tightly she would be bruised. The bed shook beneath the ferocity of his movements. The room filled with his fevered grunts as he drove faster and faster into her.

Her frantic cries joined his. "Oh, oh, oh…Thomas!" she screamed and felt Rowan's tender fingers stroking the side of her face. It only added to her pleasure.

As Gloriana fought to regain her breath, Thomas roared unintelligibly. He held her firmly in place and poured his hot cream deep within her. It seemed to go on and on. She felt the wonder of it, and then worried that he didn't know he hadn't pulled out of her as he'd been doing of late. She didn't want to tell him, and yet she had to.

In the next second, he collapsed over her. One sweaty body to another. She tried desperately not to crush Rowan and hurt his healing ribs. Reluctantly, warily, she said, "You did not pull out this time, husband."

Thomas was quiet a second, and then he eased from her body. He lifted her off Rowan and turned her to face him. Regret shown in his expression. "I was a fool, my love. Can you forgive me?"

"A fool? Forgive you?" Tears filled her eyes, clogged her throat. "What say you, my lord?"

"He tells you, our precious Glori, that he has finally changed his mind," Rowan stated.

Thomas shot him a frown and then heaved a sigh. "Rowan is right."

He caught her gaze once more. "I wish to have a daughter, with blonde hair and green eyes. I wish her to have your spirit, your gentle ways. Your stubbornness." "Well, that was certainly sappy," Rowan said with a chuckle. Gloriana gave him a glare even as she sniffed back a tear. "I am not stubborn, husband."

Both men snorted.

She lightly punched Thomas in the stomach, looking toward Rowan. "You will get your punch once your ribs have fully healed."

Then she drew in a steadying breath. "I understand your fears now, Thomas. They were more about being a father, a good father, than to do with Sarah dying." When he looked ready to interrupt, she shook her head. "Aye, it was hard her dying in childbirth. But you believed yourself a bad father—like your father—because you left James to your sister's care all these years."

She touched his face, stroked his beard stubble. "Only a *good* father would have made such a hard choice. You were not ready. You did not know how to give him a good home, but your sister could do so until you could. You may have your differences with Gavin, but you knew him to be an honorable man. He would watch after your son until you could, this you knew as well."

"I am not nearly as fine a man as you make me out to be," Thomas said quietly.

She smiled. "Again we disagree. But I will show you just how good a man I believe you to be. I will help you be the father you wish to be."

Her gaze moved to Rowan. "And I will make *you* finally see that you are far more than a cast-aside son of a foolish duke. You are worthy of anyone's love and respect." Now she took Thomas's hand and touched Rowan's leg. "We have all struggled with pains in the past, many pains. Yet somehow we found each other. I feel so very blessed." She released them and gently laid her hands over her flat stomach.

She hoped the happiness she felt showed on her face as she said, "Would you be opposed to a second son, Thomas? To our first child together, my loves?"

Thomas's eyes widened and then he tugged her to him. "You will *not* die in birthing. You hear me? You *cannot* die."

Gloriana wasn't sure how Rowan had managed to get to them so quickly, but he wrapped his arms about them both. She smiled at him. "I will not die giving you both our child. Twould not be possible. Neither of you would allow it."

Rowan smiled back. "Nay, we would not allow it."

Thomas pulled back enough to ask in concern, "What of James? He is worried that you will forget him when you have a child of your own."

She shook her head. "Never. Even though I have yet to meet my *first* son, James *will always be* my first son. Our first son."

The pleasure and relief that moved over his face touched her heart. It appeared that she had a lot of work ahead of her. All of her men—young and older—needed much reassuring, much love. Twas a very good thing she had much love to give.

The End

## About the author

Starla Kaye wears many hats professionally and as a writer. She is the community coordinator for a Midwestern accounting firm, a gerontologist who volunteers with an active group of senior adults, a mentor/teacher of writing, and a multi-published author. She dabbles in writing romances of many sub-genres: contemporary, historical Western, medieval, sci-fi, fantasy, paranormal, and Regency. To date she has published 20 novels, 37 novellas, 7 anthologies, and 15 short stories.

## Also by Starla Kaye

### Holly's Big Bad Santa

Jared had left Danville, Kansas thirteen years ago determined to never look back. He'd hurt too many people and believed he couldn't go home again. He's a much harder man now and at a turning point in his life, filled with uncertainty.

Holly has decided to let go of the past and begin a new life in California. She'd loved Jared most of her life, but she was finally giving up hope of him returning home. Even if he did, neither of them were the same people who'd been in love all those years back. He'd made his decision to leave his family and her behind. She was making hers now. Another man wants her to be with him and she aches to be loved again.

As he is recovering from nearly dying, Jared he receives a message from his parents. They want him to come home for the holidays. And they tell him the young woman he'd once loved is preparing to leave town forever. Right or wrong, he can't continue to stay away. He has to make peace with Holly and with his family.

But is it too late?

Other titles by Starla Kaye

Her Cowboy's Way
Cowboys in Charge

Latest titles from Black Velvet Seductions

Her Sister's Keeper by Leslie McKelvey
Playing By His Rules by Glenda Horsfall
Sympathy Dance by Sue McConnell
The White Spider of Savignac by V. L. Smith

See more of our titles at
www.blackvelvetseductions.com

Our titles are available from:
Amazon
Smashwords
LuLu
Nook
and other retailers

www.ingramcontent.com/pod-product-compliance
Lightning Source LLC
Chambersburg PA
CBHW030530020726
47494CB00004B/1294